ILIYA ENGLIN

Ghost of an Executioner

A Novel

EnglinSolutions ® 2006

*Distributed in association
with www.amazon.com*

Cover art – Apotheosis of War, Vasily Vereschagin, 1871

Lena,

*This was inspired by
something you once said.*

*Be more careful with
what you inspire.*

♥

Prologue

"May devil take me," rasped Sergeant Grishin, leaning out of the front hatch.

His head just visible above an untidy roll of cable strapped to the armour, Grishin squinted into binoculars and quickly withdrew inside.

"I think we found them, Comrade Major."

"Where?" asked Mironov in a tank behind, his voice indistinct from chewing on a piece of hard bread.

"On the ridge at two o'clock," replied Grishin over noisy static.

Mironov took field glasses from the shelf and made his way forward, angrily slamming the useless periscope tube with his elbow. Most of his tanks lost their periscopes to little more than vibration, and mechanics were dubious about finding replacements in the near future.

He opened the front hatch just enough to poke his binoculars outside. Training the lenses in the specified direction, he saw tiny figures move across grey-brown scree, a little more than half-way up the slope towering over the narrow valley.

They nearly made their escape in the night, he reflected, the pass to the next valley being only a few kilometres ahead. But as tough as these

Afghans were, they couldn't work miracles. Dawn caught them an impossible distance from the pass – impossible because his five tanks would now move to cut off their path and shell them into the next world.

It would be over well before the sun rose above the slope on which these Afghans would meet their inevitable and senseless deaths.

He picked up the microphone, other hand making rounds in the air through the hatch as a signal to start engines. Some of the radios went silent without warning, and men who saw action they did not understand would have orders shouted to them from an adjacent tank.

As with periscopes, radio parts took many weeks to arrive. It was easy to become very resentful if one paid attention to these small outrages, and wise men did their best to ignore them.

"Good morning, ladies," declared Mironov into the microphone. "Time to get your pretty hands dirty. The *Duhi* are on the ridge at two o'clock, range approximately two clicks. We will advance a little to optimize the range and shell them to dust. I hope it's not too much trouble to aim properly this time."

Mironov glanced upwards to assess the position of the sun as his tank shuddered forward, cold engine billowing a cloud of unburnt diesel. Raising the field glasses to his eyes, he saw tiny figures double their speed and spread around the slope.

He expected the last transmission to be as clear to the enemy as he hoped it was to his men, but that no longer mattered – it was too late for guerillas to escape. They did not have enough time to get to the pass at the end of the valley, and it was impossible for them to climb over the top of the ridge, even if they ditched what Mironov expected them to be carrying.

The tanks clattered forward, fearsome rasp of their tracks resonant in the crystal cold of Panshiri dawn. His gunner slapped a shrapnel round into the barrel, and the machinist readied the large-calibre machine gun.

Mironov tried to maintain the tiny figures in his field of vision but the tank rocked as it rumbled over the rocky valley floor. Even a man of his strength and experience found it impossible to keep the heavy binoculars still.

He swallowed the last of his bread and washed it down with a swig of evil-smelling water from the metal canister, wincing at the aftertaste that resembled stale kerosene. He had ordered his men not to leave the machines at night, something they did to collect water flowing from the mountains in the abundance of late spring. Leading by example, he too drank the awful fluid they brought from the base until it was safe to stop for such trivia, and he never hurried to consider anywhere safe. Mironov opined that no aesthetic experience was worth a sniper's bullet.

The water set him in a suitable mood for what was to come. Tanks rapidly closed the distance to where the valley floor steeply rose towards the narrow saddle of the distant pass, and Mironov toggled his microphone, ordering the column to stop.

Five T-72 tanks veered into battle formation and swung their turrets towards Mujahaddin, still barely visible amid dull-coloured rocks. Mironov blocked his ears.

"Fire," he uttered mildly.

Five heavy guns erupted in fury, their payloads slamming into the slope hundreds of meters away. The target zone disappeared in a cloud of dust, larger rocks erupting high over the slope and raining down on those still seeking shelter in its wounded contour.

"Again," ordered Mironov, studying the slope intently.

He watched as shells exploded amid the dust, thunder of their explosions shaking the entire valley.

"Move in closer," he said into the microphone. "Let's say half-way, then widen the formation."

The tanks veered into a wider row and clattered towards the slope slowly. The drivers were frantically focussed on the ground ahead, seeking signs of rock cover being at all disturbed to plant mines. It seemed an impossible task, yet most tank drivers got good at it eventually – if they lived long enough.

When they neared the rise of the slope Mironov stopped them and scanned the mountain through the front hatch.

Once the dust was carried away by the stiff mountain breeze he was able to see the bodies in his binoculars – seeing mostly what was left of them. He systematically scanned the slope for any rock large enough to conceal a man, then directed fire to each potential hideout.

One shell slammed into a hastily constructed mound of boulders and sent a geyser of rock over the slope. Mironov was then rewarded by another explosion that temporarily blotted out the view with a burst of bright orange, followed by a shower of rock debris.

"See that, damsels?" asked Mironov into the

microphone proudly. "Those were the famous Stinger missiles. You are looking at this region's heroin crop going up in smoke, and there are now a dozen helicopters, maybe, whose crews will see their mothers again."

He heard the cheer in other tanks join that of his crew. American heat-seeking missiles were the worst weapon in the hands of stoic primitives, a seemingly indestructible people who melted into the ground at the approach of Soviet troops, only to reappear behind the attackers and take their toll on the cream of his country's youth.

When news came of the latest shipments, one making it nearly all the way across the country to the Soviet border, Mironov's unit was chosen for excellent reasons. His men were older than most soldiers serving in this miserable country, by now professionals who performed far above mere conscripts, and Mironov was not a run-of-the-mill Soviet commander. In this theatre his individuality was considered a positive quality.

He lectured his troops repeatedly, telling them that it is up to better men than he to explain why the Afghan campaign is run along its present lines and why they were in Afghanistan to begin with. But given that they were busily stirring this nest of wasps, it was a good idea to keep the action away from Soviet borders.

That usually involved hunting down the highly mobile Mujahaddin units and blowing them to dust, not the least because adjacent Soviet provinces were populated by millions of Muslims.

For over a century Russia had absolute control in its Central Asian domains. They were torn from decaying Persia with ease – but it was belatedly realized that the seemingly docile Soviet subjects were close relatives of die-hards on the other side of the Afghan border. It was yet another fire hazard that was contemptuously ignored by those who started the war.

The cloud now cleared, and Mironov could see that his job was done. Nothing was left alive on the slope – whoever lived through the shelling could not have survived the final explosion, the American missiles cooking off their fuel and payload at once.

"Good work," he said into the microphone. "Turn around and head back, ladies. You might get breakfast in bed if you hurry."

He leaned back to change frequencies and increased the wattage.

"Headquarters MR-1210, respond," he said into the microphone, still scanning the slopes of the valley as his tank turned to lead the column.

"MR-1210 receiving," crackled the voice in his

headphones.

"MR-1210, this is Major Mironov reporting," replied Mironov in a robotic monotone which semi-powerful people in the Soviet Union used on official business.

"Coordinates three-five-two-seven-five-five slash six-nine-five-nine-five-six, bandit unit ambushed with a quantity American missiles. Bandits and missiles destroyed. No losses. Now returning to base. Over."

"Report acknowledged, Comrade Major," replied the distant voice. "Duty officer will be informed immediately."

Mironov returned to the frequency used as an intercom by his group.

"Proceed to base," he ordered wearily.

He slumped back in his seat, wondering if there was any point in sleeping before they returned. The night before was tense as always – lying in wait for the enemy in open country was a calculated gamble with all lives present. It was not impossible to sneak up on tanks and plant enough explosive to damage the tracks. Then kerosene was poured into the engine bay and set on fire, incinerating the crew.

"Comrade Major," said the radio operator. "It's

the base."

Mironov sat up and flicked the switch on the unit above him.

"Major Mironov receiving," he barked irritably.

"Major Mironov, this is Captain Mashkin, duty officer," replied an agitated baritone. "Restate your position and course immediately."

Mironov spread the map on his knee and squinted at the contour of the valley. He estimated his coordinates as honestly as he could and relayed them twice.

"Stand by," ordered Mashkin. A long pause ensued.

"Idiots," mumbled Mironov holding his hand over the microphone.

"Captain Mashkin transmitting," proclaimed the baritone. "Stand by to receive new orders."

"Yes, standing by," replied Mironov with a heavy frown.

There was a short pause then the radio crackled again.

"Turn around and proceed to bearing one-eighty," said Mashkin. Destination coordinates one-four-three-four-nine. You are required to secure the pass and the next valley."

Mironov didn't react immediately. He stared at the map, rechecking grid references, but came up with the same answer again and again.

"Comrade Major, acknowledge," demanded Mashkin.

"I acknowledge, *tvou mat'*!" shouted Mironov. "We can't go back there, *mudak* – every *Duh* in the area is headed this way. We just killed a few dozen of their relatives, don't you understand?"

"These are your new orders," replied Mashkin blandly.

"From?" barked Mironov, his stomach turning cold with fear.

"One minute, Comrade Major."

There was a lengthy pause during which Mironov switched frequencies and ordered his column to stop. He then returned to await clarification.

"The order came from Lieutenant-General Berezov," replied Mashkin.

"Get this back to him right now," growled

Mironov, fighting back panic. "We only have five tanks, and we will get slaughtered at that pass. The bastards simply have to be there – that's where the missiles were going!"

"Stand by, Comrade Major," replied Mashkin with a total lack of concern.

Mironov glanced at the sun, now high above the valley. It melted the night cold with its caresses, taking away any ice that may have slowed down the guerrillas in the hills.

"This is Captain Mashkin," announced the baritone sententiously. "Comrade General was not pleased to repeat his order. Proceed as instructed immediately. Out."

Mironov immediately switched frequencies.

"Ladies," he said urgently. "We just got a new set of orders. Don't ask me why, but we have to go back south through that pass."

There was no reply but he saw the faces inside the cabin grow pale. His tank rolled to a stop, indicating that the tank in front has done likewise.

"How, Major?" asked the Sergeant Grishin, in charge of the lead tank.

"In our classically heroic spirit," replied Mironov

acidly. "Just don't sing, whatever else you do."

There was complete silence, broken only by an even throb of fully warmed diesels in idle as he thought.

"All right," he said into the microphone steadily. "We load up every gun now and go at top speed, column formation. You see anyone – send them straight to Allah. Repeat – fire at will, any time, any target. Now turn around and let's go, devil spawn."

The machines swung around and returned to the original column formation, accelerating amid clouds of dust and blue exhaust smoke. Mironov opened the top hatch a little wider than usual and studied the pass for the first time.

Closer to the pass the valley became a gorge between two jagged mountain slopes. Its floor was creased by a stream that scored its way through bedrock, and a rough road wound alongside the river up to the pass.

All drivers followed the road but kept five metres to the right, knowing that anything that looked like a path in Afghanistan was mined by all warring sides.

They were progressing well even as the rising slope made their tanks labour and spit rocks from the treads. T-72 is capable of running at forty-five kilometres an hour over moderately rough terrain, and they appeared to be averaging close to top speed. Mironov estimated that the pass was some two kilometres away, quickly calculating that the danger – or their lives – should end within minutes.

He still couldn't see anything that looked like an ambush, and one part of him prayed to a God he was not supposed to know, to ask that just this once things would be as they appeared.

He craved nothing less than a lucky break. If he didn't get it, it was difficult to see how they could survive that sunny morning. They all knew better than submit to capture, and anyone trapped by the enemy would fight to the death.

The saddle of the pass was already in clear sight, and Mironov frantically scanned the path as it ran alongside the river, its flow now a shallow trickle glittering among rocks of dull grey. He saw not a single trace of anything untoward. The harsh sun bore down onto the slopes, and he hoped that little could be hidden in such clear light.

It was a thought that he finished with his body flung upwards, the entire tank being tossed into the air. The machine landed heavily, noise from the front sprocket a sure sign that the explosion blew off the right track.

Rocket-propelled grenades whistled their lethal

song as they arced into the gorge from the slopes above. Many men were hidden there with expertise that defied Mironov's vision entirely.

The first tank in the column erupted into flames – then its hatches were blasted into the air by exploding ammunition. A shower of shrapnel sprayed the front of Mironov's tank, and he smelt the deathly bouquet of burning cordite, diesel and flesh.

The last two tanks also took hits, but these projectiles bounced harmlessly over armour, exploding further on. The tank behind Mironov survived a hit at the base of its turret, but its traverse gears jammed, denying it the ability to swivel its turret to fire at side targets. The other three tanks rained return fire, spreading lead over slopes surrounding the pass.

Mironov tried the front hatch but it was now jammed. He dropped out through the bottom hatch and stole a fast glance from beneath to assess the situation.

His gunners fired wildly in all directions, but it seemed to Mironov that they succeeded in laying down enough suppressing fire. He pulled back up to reach for the microphone just as a few bullets chipped rocks near his head. He felt a sting on his cheek and ignored it entirely.

"Grishin, Leflkovich," he ordered. "Surround my flanks. Komarov, get into the stream and reverse closer to us. We will try to get out underneath."

It was a manoeuvre he never hoped to implement in battle. As his crippled machine was flanked by two intact tanks laying down covering fire, the third reversed into the entire formation and stopped in front of the crippled tank to cover the path of escaping men.

Hearing steel plates collide roughly, Mironov ordered out his crew through the bottom hatch. They hurriedly crawled to the tank in front of them and started to climb into its entrails. He threw down the microphone and moved towards the hatch to follow them.

Then the tank just bordered by his crew exploded with sufficient force to blow off the turret. Mironov was thrown against the turret wall by the blast, hitting his head hard against the steel. The helmet stopped his skull from breaking, but he was blinded by stars for a few minutes and waited for it to pass.

When his vision returned Mironov saw that he was trapped by one burning tank in front and another behind. Trying the top hatch was suicide – if he didn't die from a well-aimed bullet, the flames would probably prove lethal, judging by the rapidly rising temperature in his tank.

That left only one course of action.

"Grishin, Leflkovich!" he shouted into the microphone. "Go."

He touched the traverse lever and was relieved as his turret rotated slightly in response. He loaded another round into the gun and fired into the slope from where the last missile appeared to have originated.

"Major!" shouted Grishin from the tank on his left in horror.

"Go!!!" screamed Mironov at the top of his voice. He didn't use the radio, but they heard him over the flames.

"Comrade Major," repeated Grishin. "I am going to ram the tank in front of you and push it a short distance. You can then evacuate."

Mironov dove to the floor and grasped the microphone.

"As you were!" he screamed. "It's too late to get me out! Go, fuck it, go!"

"Major!" was the desperate reply. It was drowned by an explosion as another missile bounced over Mironov's hull and detonated on the ground nearby.

A small electrical fire sprang from the corner of the driver's console, blue flames sending an acrid stench into the stale air of the cabin. Mironov coughed and threw an asbestos blanket over the instruments. The flames diminished but continued to dance behind the panel.

Mironov sat up and leaned against a warm armoured wall, now at peace. He knew that his lifespan was now measurable in minutes and saw no reason to spoil what little he had.

"Listen," he mouthed into the microphone quietly. "I'm as good as gone. All I can do is cover your retreat."

There was no reply, and he took a deep breath.

"Now go – or I will die for nothing. And no talk."

The radio remained silent as engines were gunned to the hilt. Both machines left his flanks and tore up the pass, still firing around them at random. Mironov ratcheted the slide of the heavy machine gun and began to cover the slope systematically, rotating the turret as he fired. The guerrillas remained hidden, patiently waiting for him to run out of ammunition.

By the time he stopped firing the other tanks cleared the saddle of the pass and disappeared behind over the horizon. The *Duhi* emerged from the rocks and approached at a steady pace as Mironov's guns stared at them in silence.

Mironov tore the cover off a shell magazine and located an incendiary round. He then cracked open the top hatch to watch as guerrillas surrounded his machine – around a hundred men, all dressed in a ragged mixture of camouflage and traditional Afghan clothing and heavily armed. They held their weapons aloft and waited for the crew to emerge, maintaining complete silence and calm.

Mironov pulled out his service pistol and chambered a round, taking off the safety catch with his thumb. He hesitated, forcing himself to remember the last time he had felt like a normal human being.

It was when he managed to get away in the second year of the war, he decided. He was granted leave to return to Moscow for New Year, which he spent with his sole relative – an elderly aunt, who usually put on a wild party.

Images jostled in his mind.

A cramped lounge room with a fragrant fir tree, set in a tub dressed in white cloth. Black and white TV blaring a corny variety show. Good food procured from nowhere despite the choking shortages. The Kremlin clock striking midnight on TV, then an eruption of cold champagne that topped off the long night's river of vodka.

He remembered waking up before dawn and coming out onto the balcony to relight a stale cigarette. He especially revelled in the memory of intense cold that crawled under the greatcoat loosely draped over his body. Mironov shivered involuntarily as he recalled rubbing his face and neck with light, powdery snow that covered the balcony overnight, to chase away the last vodka fumes.

He smiled at the memory of a girl with whom he shared the previous night, a junior colleague of his aunt's. They improvised a bed of sofa cushions in the tiny kitchen, making the most of other merrymakers' reluctance to rise early.

He recalled how New Year's first dawn broke over Moscow to the muffled sounds of traffic stirring amid dense snow. He recalled the sounds of ubiquitous old women scraping paths after the blizzard had ushered in a new decade.

Later that morning he rubbed his chest under a hot shower until he was fully awake. When he emerged, rough uniform cloth prickly against hot skin, others were already up and about, smells of frying eggs and coffee drifting from the kitchen.

After breakfast he and his friend took to the nearby Izmailovskiy Park on hastily borrowed skis.

They ambled along in the perfect purity of cold air, sun shining through a thin cloud that still sprinkled sparkling snowflakes. He remembered the feel of frost on his cheeks, the smell of fir trees dressed in white, the sound of snow creaking under wooden skis.

A gentle smile creased the mask of blood and soot that was Mironov's face. He raised the pistol and fired point-blank into the primer of an incendiary shell.

The remaining ammunition detonated at once, convulsing the mountains with thunder. The blast's fury shredded tired armour, spraying the Mujahaddin with razor shards of hardened steel. Most died instantly, a few unlucky men surviving longer with deep wounds and macerated eyes.

The fuel tank miraculously survived the explosion and was tossed into the air intact. It burst as it landed, diesel igniting on contact with white-hot phosphorus spilled from incendiary shells.

Dense fuel burned as it spread over rocky ground. A column of acrid smoke drifted on a breeze across the valley – worthy incense for an altar where honour, insanity and futility were worshipped side by side.

Part I

His train slowly pulled into the station, exhaust-stained carriages companions to the faded and peeling paint of the once-beautiful building. The metal doors slid open, and the platform's press turned to pandemonium as people dragged poorly packaged luggage through narrow doors. Relatives squealed, uniforms strolled and others stood still, crowd flowing around them.

As the flow from the train began to subside, a man of average height with sandy hair cut very short emerged from the lead carriage. He was dressed in a crisply pressed uniform of a Guards officer and easily carried a large battered suitcase in his right hand.

There was nothing unusual about this officer as he strutted the length of the platform except his eyes. Sunken deep into a gaunt face, they were open wide as if in shock or profound pain, grey-blue irises a severe contrast to the red and swollen lids.

He slowly walked out of the train station and crossed the square to enter a small park. As soon as he made it to the first bench he sat down, not bothering to brush the coat of snow from faded boards. His head bowed down, and he sat still, the shoulders trembling beneath the heavy greatcoat.

He stayed still for a long time, then the shuddering slowly subsided. He wiped his eyes without raising his head and ran his hands through the snow.

"Major," he heard a young voice beside him and looked up.

He saw two young soldiers on patrol, their winter uniforms creased and boots scuffed. They wore their weapons around the right shoulder, as per regulation, but the number of ammunition pouches on their wide belts left no doubt as to what they were prepared for in broad daylight, right in the centre of Moscow.

"As you were, lads," he stood up and returned their salute.

"Are you all right, Comrade Major?" asked the dark-haired soldier with wide Asiatic cheekbones.

"Yes, son," replied the officer. "A long journey with bad sleep, nothing more."

"Do you have someone to meet you?" asked the soldier.

"Oh – no. I was going to take a taxi to my relative's house."

"That may be difficult, Comrade Major," said the second soldier. "It's getting late for taxis – we are expecting trouble here."

"Trouble?" asked the officer, now totally bewildered. "What kind of trouble?"

"The usual," the first soldier replied. "Mafia battles. The Mozhinsky mob hired an entire de-mobbed squad of marines last week. We figure they will finish drinking and whoring any day now – and then they have scores to settle from here to Japan. We make sure nobody gets caught out here after dark."

"I see," replied the officer in a neutral tone. "This is all a little new to me, lads. I served overseas for a long time."

"Yes Comrade Major," said the second soldier. "We will call you one of the supply cars. They can give you a ride to some place safe."

"Much obliged," replied the officer. "Good work, lads."

They summoned a *UAZ*, a squat Soviet version of the Jeep, which arrived within minutes. He returned their salutes and got into the back seat, the front being stacked with boxes filled with coarse rye bread. Mironov was completely bewildered to see that the *UAZ* was driven by a civilian, an older man with a red band around his right arm.

"Where do you need to go, *Gospodin Ofitzer*?" asked the driver.

He mouthed the address, startled by the greeting.

"Not far," commented the driver. "I'll take you there."

The officer nodded his thanks, and they accelerated down a wide street flanked with dirty snow. He stared around wildly.

Gospodin. Mother of God. Not Comrade, but *Gospodin*, a pre-revolutionary form of address that was banned in Russia for more than seventy years.

But that was only a hint of surprises to follow. They drove past a police station, and the officer saw that the bottom of its wide staircase was stacked with two semicircles of sandbags, behind which he saw two large-calibre machine gun emplacements. He stared at the helmeted heads of soldiers manning the guns behind sandbags.

The officer was even more startled to see a line of ragged dents left in the soft masonry by automatic fire. But the biggest shock came when he looked up to see the flags flying from two masts set in the wall on either side of the entrance.

"White on blue on red," he whispered. "My God."

"Excuse me?" asked the driver.

"Oh, nothing," replied his passenger hurriedly. "Just trying to remember something. Say, why have they put machine gun emplacements here?"

"Oh, that was the militia station," said the driver with contempt. "It was attacked last week."

"What?"

"Repin's crowd. They arrested one of them and held him overnight at the station instead of shipping him off to the base like they were supposed to."

"Sounds like a mistake," suggested the officer sarcastically.

"Sure was," said the driver. "Eight people died in the night attack, including two of Mozhinsky's men."

"And the man they arrested?"

"Killed by his pals right in his cell," replied the driver, curving his mouth. "Some liberation. Didn't want him talking, I suppose."

"Right," said the officer, completely confused.

The driver's eyes shot to the rear view mirror and assessed his passenger.

"Have you been away a long time?"

"Yes," replied the officer. "*Afgan*, then…other places."

"I see," replied the driver. "You will find that everything is very different now."

"You're right about that," said the officer. "Lord…"

"You want to be careful," commented the driver sadly. "Your relatives, are they well set up?"

"Ah..." replied the officer hesitantly. "I think I know what you mean. No. It's just one elderly aunt."

"I understand," said the driver thoughtfully.

They arrived to the house the officer recognized immediately. It hasn't changed, he noted gratefully, as the *UAZ* drove inside a courtyard enclosed by four apartment buildings and stopped outside a grimy entrance. The light was beginning to fade.

The officer stepped out and shut the door. He was surprised to see the elderly man get out of the vehicle and come around, looking in all directions.

"Come with me," he whispered, walking into the entrance. The officer followed him.

When they were inside, the driver handed him an

object wrapped in a soiled oily rag. The officer unwrapped it and looked up sharply.

"Is it that bad?" he demanded curtly.

"Worse," answered the driver. "What I would really recommend is a machine pistol – but this is all I have to give. Please take it – the boys confiscate them all the time, and I will get another tomorrow. It has a full clip."

The officer nodded slowly and extended his right hand. The driver shook it and hurried out of the doorway.

After watching him drive off the officer turned and mounted a short flight of greasy steps towards the lift. As he waited for the ancient contraption to arrive, he checked the pistol.

It was an older Makarov, but well-cleaned and in good condition. He tucked it inside his trousers and stepped into the lift, stabbing the button for the eighth floor.

He emerged from the lift, familiar smells of boiled cabbage and stale fat tickling his nostrils. Now deep inside the apartment building, he felt its reassurance. The dim lighting and the damp, warm air that wafted up the stairwell were the same as when he last walked that stained floor. At that point reality was that of rigid control that he and his masters exercised entirely.

He hesitated for a moment, straightened his tie and rang his aunt's bell.

There was a lengthy pause, then a light flashed in the viewer crudely set into the solid wood of the door. A lock clicked, and the door opened slightly.

A young man stared at him with cold suspicion across the chain.

"Yes?"

"I am Maria Fedorovna's nephew," stated the officer neutrally.

"Whose?" asked the young man with even greater hostility.

"Maria Fedorovna," repeated the officer.

"Wait... I know," affirmed the young man. "Show me your papers."

The officer hesitated at the insolence of that request, but lifelong instinct took over. He opened his greatcoat and slowly retrieved his military passport from its inside pocket. The young man took it without a word and shut the door.

There was a long delay, then a flurry of male

voices behind the door. It was opened again to reveal a thin middle-aged man in an ill-fitting suit. For a few moments he stared at the visitor over his grey moustache stained with tobacco, compared him with the picture in the passport and handed the document back.

"Major Viktor Maratovich Mironov," he greeted the visitor politely. "My name is Aleksandr Ivanovich Rebkov. Captain of the Soviet Navy, regrettably retired. Also regrettably, I have sad news for you, Major. Please come in."

The young man shut the door behind them, and Mironov set his suitcase on the floor. The young man hung up his coat on a stand near the door, then disappeared somewhere into the bowels of the flat.

Rebkov led him into the lounge room, but his visitor stopped as if electrocuted at the threshold. He stared, with abject horror, at the posters of Hitler and Stalin, both on brown background with red edges. They hung on an otherwise bare wall above what looked like a makeshift office.

"Please sit down," said Rebkov, motioning him to the chair opposite a large desk cluttered with papers. He crossed the room and sat behind the desk, shaking two cigarettes out of a crumpled packet. He offered the pack to his visitor, who shook his head. Rebkov lit one and sat back, blowing a cloud of foul smoke out of the corner of his mouth as he stared at Mironov intently.

"I regret to advise you that your aunt passed away two years ago," he announced, watching Mironov closely. "My condolences, Comrade Major."

The visitor was more confused by the surroundings than by his aunt's death, which he largely expected. He nodded slightly.

"If you are wondering, this is the regional office of the *Pamyat'* Patriotic Organization," said Rebkov. "Your late aunt was a highly committed member before her decease, and she left this flat to us in her will. I have a copy here."

He passed an official-looking sheet to his visitor, who studied it perfunctorily, nodded and handed it back.

"I hope there won't be any trouble," said Rebkov.

"No," replied Mironov grimly. "I'll be on my way, then."

He stood and replaced the chair. They walked out to the front door, where Mironov reached for his greatcoat.

"Say, Comrade," added Rebkov with a slight frost in his voice. "Isn't that the service medal for

Afgan?"

Mironov ran his fingers across the left breast, as if becoming aware of its contents for the first time. There was little left of the space allocated for decoration ribbons.

"Yes," he replied, his voice now curt and decisive, a voice that carried over air waves to guide men as if his hand held them by the collar.

"Aren't you a little young for that?" asked Rebkov with a mocking edge to his voice. "You don't look a day over thirty. Wouldn't that make you – what, fifteen, when they awarded you that decoration?"

His visitor chuckled, turning back from the door to face him. Rebkov shrunk slightly from the change in appearance – the man's eyes were now narrow slits in an armour plate.

"Here," spat Mironov, removing his passport from the pocket of his coat. He pointed to his date of birth.

Rebkov peered at it myopically and smiled.

"Congratulations on your appearance, Comrade Major," he said wistfully. "Like I said, you don't look a day over thirty. My apologies."

When his visitor picked up his suitcase and turned to the door, Rebkov offered him a stack of papers.

"Some information about our organization," he said suggestively.

"Thanks," replied his visitor neutrally. He placed the papers into the coat pocket.

They parted with curt nods rather than handshakes. As the door shut behind, Mironov walked back towards the lift, reading a brochure in hues of brown, black and red. His hand shook indignantly when he learned that Mother Russia once again called on its sons to save her from a Jewish conspiracy.

When the lift doors opened, he tossed the papers into the well.

Night all but set in as he left the apartment building. There was very little light – most of the street lamps were shattered with what looked like automatic fire.

He became aware of an unnatural silence that enveloped him in the darkness. Nothing moved, he realized more with annoyance than fear. The street appeared to be totally deserted, moonlight weaving beautiful patterns on its pleated coat of snow.

Mironov took out the pistol, chambered a round and checked the safety catch. He slid the weapon into the left sleeve of his coat, stretching the elastic band of his watch to secure the barrel on his wrist. He unbuttoned the leather glove and hid the butt of the pistol in its flare, then flicked his wrist to test a release. Satisfied, he picked up the suitcase with the right hand and walked on aimlessly.

Other streets appeared to be equally deserted. Occasionally cars passed him by, tyre noise muffled by fresh snow. Most of them appeared to be powerful-looking foreign sedans filled with men who stared at Mironov's lone figure with some surprise.

A military patrol stopped to check his papers. He explained that a relative had died during his lengthy tour of duty, which unexpectedly left him without accommodation. He would walk to Novoslobodsky *Prospekt* and catch a taxi from there.

The men of that night patrol were in a hurry and accepted his story without offering help. They drove away saying very little and left him alone in the dark.

He turned into a small alleyway that led past the grounds of a large school. He aimlessly strode towards the ugly building where his aunt had taught mathematics during a better part of her life.

Whenever he visited Moscow, Mironov was shamelessly displayed to her colleagues. She especially enjoyed wreaking havoc among young women drawn to Mironov's shapely figure, clad as he was in a heavily decorated uniform of an elite unit.

The civil defence teacher was a major too, remembered Mironov, a very short bald-headed man with massive shoulders, who walked around school in a full dress uniform. He was a rare species – a former partisan who survived Stalin's gratitude after the war. Most of them went straight to the death camps – Father of All Nations didn't like independent operators.

The Major was a rotten teacher, Mironov recalled with a smile. Handling children, even though Soviet ones obeyed orders instinctively, was not his forté. He had trouble controlling ten-year-olds he was supposed to instruct in what was essentially infantry training.

So the old soldier made deals. In exchange for mastering a satisfactory marching drill he once taught them to throw knives. Mironov went along to watch and adopted the old man's technique, which was the best he saw in his long and bloody career thick with "special assignments".

He heard agitated voices in the alley and moved into shadows instinctively. The voices came closer, and he set down his suitcase, becoming still and nearly invisible in the dark.

As they went past, Mironov saw a woman in her early thirties who limped, struggling to keep up with two men. She was dressed in a miniskirt and a short fur coat, her pageboy blond hair dishevelled and long leather boots partly unzipped. Her face radiated a china-doll beauty classic of Northern Russians, but its exquisite features were twisted with distress.

The young men she followed walked at a casual pace, their faces creased by malignant amusement. They were both of solid build and wore long leather coats, unbuttoned to reveal untidily worn suits.

"Please," she shouted hoarsely. "I need that money for my child!"

"*Zatknis', blyad'*," hissed one of the men without turning around. "You'll awaken the whole street."

She caught up with them and grasped the belt of his coat.

"What?" he frowned angrily. "Are you tired of living?"

He lazily swung his torso, flinging his arm through the air. The backhander landed on the woman's cheek, felling her backwards into the snow. She remained there, sobbing helplessly.

"Look at that," declared his companion, pointing at her splayed legs. "I think she wants some more."

They turned and stood over her. One casually kicked the inside of her calf, pushing her legs further apart.

"As you were!" barked Mironov, stepping out from the shadows. They turned in surprise.

"*Gospodin Ofitzer!*" exclaimed the man who delivered the backhander with a mock bow. "Why don't you fuck off while you still can? Go defend the Motherland somewhere."

"Here will do just fine," retorted Mironov, his voice a clatter of steel tracks. "Disappear, vermin."

Both men smiled with glee. One of them opened his coat with both hands to show Mironov a folded assault rifle strapped to his chest.

"A good weapon," said Mironov approvingly. "But too complex to maintain by garbage like you."

"How about this?" the other man casually extracted a compact machine pistol from its holster and hefted in in his hand. Mironov focussed on the finger nearest to the safety catch.

The threat only became real once that finger traversed a few centimetres – but that took a short time that one learned to use to full advantage.

"Now that I think of it, I am running late," mouthed Mironov in a hasty tone of a man who belatedly realizes being out of his depth. "What's the time, anyway?"

He casually raised his left arm and slid back its sleeve with the right hand, as if to expose his watch. The rest happened too fast for his opponents to follow.

Two shots thundered in the night's silence. Mironov stood still, listening for any reaction, then stepped closer and checked the bodies. Each had a dark hole precisely in the centre of the forehead that made checking for signs of life redundant.

Mironov went over the corpses systematically, stripping one of outer clothing. He removed wallets, expensive watches and weapons, throwing them into his largely empty suitcase. He then dragged both bodies into the dark part of the alley and turned to the woman.

She managed to get up, rubbing snow into a swelling cheekbone, and she now stared past him with an expression of terminal fatigue in which nothing matters and nothing is much of a surprise anyway.

"Do you know what you have done?" she asked hoarsely as he finished his plunder.

"Two good deeds," he replied briskly, looking up. "What was that about your money?"

She pointed to a bundle of cash tied with a rubber band, now lying on top of the dead man's clothes. He nodded and tossed it towards her.

She was completely caught by surprise, her arms twitching feebly as the bundle hit her on the chest and fell on the snow.

Wincing with pain, she slowly bent down and picked it up, then looked up at Mironov with concern.

"You are crazy, right?" she whispered with fear.

He chuckled and shut his suitcase, thinking over the reply.

"I've been away for a long time," he replied after a while. "This is my first day back in Russia."

She nodded with gathering understanding.

"A long time?" she repeated, stepping closer.

He opened his mouth, then closed it and shook his head in silence.

"Very," replied Mironov.

"You have a lot to learn," she said mournfully. "Everything is different now."

"No problem," replied Mironov, gesturing at the corpses. "I'm a good student."

"Right," announced the woman, appearing to reach a decision. "Where are you going now?"

"Away," replied Mironov. "I don't think I want to be here for much longer."

"Come with me," said the woman curtly. "Otherwise you'll be dead before dawn – the people you killed will be missed in an hour."

"And where are you going?" asked Mironov.

"Home," she answered, pointing at a tall building a few streets away. "It's safe."

He nodded.

They covered that distance slowly, the woman increasingly favouring her left leg. He moved in closer as she slowed down and half-lifted her by her right arm.

They eventually reached the vestibule of a tall concrete slab, the likes of which sprouted all over the Eastern Bloc to house its cowering multitudes – tiny rabbit warren flats with bad plumbing and uncertain heating. The woman extracted her keys and opened a heavy metal grill, crudely installed across the entrance. It looked more like a barricade than a peacetime installation.

The warmth inside carried the signature scent of a Russian apartment building – two parts of stale cooking to one part of sweat, garbage and tobacco, in proportions dependent on local circumstances.

They made it to the lift, the woman leaning more and more on his arm. With three steps to go, she started to cry with pain. Mironov picked her up with his free hand and carried her into the lift.

She slid down his torso with a tiny moan of pain and pressed a button, her hands remaining around his neck for support. They rode up to the top of the building in silence. As the lift stopped, he picked her up again and carried her to the door of her flat.

She fumbled with keys, then Mironov pushed open the door, and set her down on the floor gently. She locked the door with her key, leaving it in the lock, and limped away, throwing her coat off and trailing it along the floor.

He followed her into the tiny flat, sparsely but neatly furnished. She made it to the couch in the corner of the lounge room and sank down with a cry of pain.

Mironov knelt in front of her, placing his hands on her right knee. She lifted her short skirt to show him a massive bruise on her inner thigh. He could see where the sophisticated tread of an expensive boot crushed her white skin.

She was naked under her patterned stockings. Ignoring this completely, he checked the extent of the bruise and nodded curtly, then went to the kitchen and returned with a plastic bag. He stepped out the door onto a tiny balcony and filled the bag with snow. His expert hands spun the bag to shut it tight and pressed it to the bruise.

She gasped at its cold but stayed still, small drops of sweat appearing on her forehead. Her hands dropped onto the bag and pressed it to the injury.

"Vodka," uttered Mironov mildly.

She pointed towards a cabinet under the small television set. He marched there and poured a large slug of vodka into a wine glass. Returning to the couch, he held the rim of the glass to her mouth.

Surprised by the quantity she choked on the fiery liquid, spilling only a few drops. Mironov placed the glass on the floor under the sofa and went to hang his greatcoat near the door.

When he returned she looked in less pain, her hands turning white with cold on the plastic bag. He took it away and replenished the snow, this time pressing it to her thigh as he knelt beside her.

"Thank you," she whispered hoarsely. "I am not cut out for what I do."

He looked up sharply.

"And that is?" he asked with a frown.

"I can see you've been away soldiering for a long time," she said with a grim chuckle.

"That's right," he replied in a level tone. "Care to enlighten me?"

"I whore," she spat vehemently. "*Dyra na prokat.* Slot for hire, all right?"

He acknowledged the statement with a curt nod.

"Sorry you bothered helping me now?" she asked caustically.

"No," he shook his head grimly. "I am not one to judge you."

He released his hold on the plastic bag and stood up abruptly, turning away from her.

"I am not one to judge anybody," he said, his voice turning hoarse. "Not after what I've done in my life."

"What was that?" she asked, her vehemence receding.

"I killed for the Soviet Union," he replied, turning towards her and pointing to his decoration ribbons. "They gave me all these for what I've done. Understand?"

"I heard stories," she confirmed sadly. "My class was the last to go to *Afgan*. The ones who returned didn't want to talk about it much, and what they did talk about I didn't want to hear."

Mironov shuddered slightly and let out an explosive breath. His face a pallid mask, he furiously wiped his eyes with a sleeve and sat down at a dinner table, which occupied most of the room.

"I am not one to judge you," he repeated. "I am glad I was in that alley."

"I am too," she replied, belligerence now gone from her voice.

They sat in silence for a while, then he replaced the snow in her bag. The swelling was now going down, and colour returned to her face.

"Did you live in Moscow?" she asked.

"Not for a long time."

"There is going to be trouble," she said. "We have to be careful."

"I just need a few hours' sleep," countered Mironov. "I can be gone by dawn."

"Right," she said tiredly. "We will sort this out in the morning."

She rose to her feet, placed weight on her right leg experimentally and limped to the corridor. He followed her to a tiny bedroom, which smelled strongly of an antiseptic.

She turned on the light and Mironov was startled to see a profusion of toys, posters of animals and bright furniture. She motioned to a narrow bed, which was tightly made up.

"Sleep here," she said, closing the door behind her.

***

Mironov awoke late, dim light of the northern morning seeping through a soot-stained window. He dressed and made his bed before venturing from the bedroom, spent a while washing his face and hands in the bathroom, then followed the signs of life to the kitchen.

She sat behind the tiny table holding a cup of coffee, dressed in a thick white gown, her blond hair now in place. There was a hint of make-up on her face, which brought out the deep blue of her eyes with stunning effect.

"You sleep a long time for a soldier," she said lightly.

"No great hurry," replied Mironov evenly. "What's your name?"

"Nina", she replied. "Sit down, you need to eat."

"Just some bread," he asked, sitting down. "And water."

Nina sniffed derisively.

"Are you religious or something?"

"No," he replied. "That's just what I want to eat."

"Can't tempt you with eggs and sausages?"

"No."

She put a plate in front of him and cut off three pieces of rye bread.

He nodded his thanks and ate, washing down the bread with tap water.

When he finished, she took away his plate and sat on the kitchen bench opposite him.

"Are you married?" she asked.

"No."

"A woman some place?"

"No."

"Good," she said. "I'd like to thank you for last night."

She began to unbutton her gown. He watched motionlessly as she got down to her stomach, revealing smooth pale skin flanked by the swell of generous breasts.

"Not necessary," he replied, waving her away. An expression of surprise spread over her face.

"I don't like being in debt," she said, slowly pulling the gown apart.

"You aren't." He stood up and closed her gown firmly.

"Oh," she stuttered awkwardly. "Are you… *goluboi*?"

"No," he chuckled grimly at this almost-polite reference to being gay. "There is nothing wrong with you, either. I just don't need to."

"Okay," she buttoned up the gown. "Then tell me why you are here."

"It's a long story," he replied.

"I don't like the sound of that," she replied, pouring herself another coffee from the pot. "It sounds like trouble."

"You're right," he replied. "I need to find some people."

"I definitely don't like the sound of that," said Nina.

"It's not your problem," replied Mironov. "I'll be on my way."

"Where?" asked Nina with pointed irony.

Mironov stopped in mid-breath to assess this question. He acknowledged that he didn't know the answer, being in a totally alien environment without any idea how to proceed.

"There's a bit of a problem," said Nina. "If you show yourself out there, you'll be done for."

She motioned him to the window. Mironov followed and looked out with a sense of weary dread.

The street was alive with police and military uniforms, flashing blue lights slicing the muted winter daylight. He guessed more than saw that their attention was centred on the site of his kill, and he turned to her with consternation.

"You shouldn't leave for a day or two," she explained. "You are a stranger, and you will be recognized right away. Then they will search you and find the dead men's things."

"Who were they?" he asked, the spell broken. An operational plan had to be devised, quickly. It was bound to require some bold and unexpected action on his part. Nothing was so alien after all.

"Repin's spivs," she replied. "Repin is ex-KGB. He now owns this area."

"How?" he asked with amazement.

"Simple," she shrugged. "He sat outside the

barracks when shock troops were brought back from East Germany and demobilized. He promised to actually pay them for work so they could put food in front of their families. That's how they left the army with all their weapons to do his business: drugs, under-age girls, protection and guns. He is a very wealthy man, and he owns this sector."

"Right," he uttered slowly, having digested that information.

"Those two pulled me over last night," she said tonelessly. "Forced me to service them in their car. Then they searched me and found the money, which they took. I really need it."

"Does anyone know you were with them?" he asked.

"No," she replied. "They hide their limousine in a garage behind the school. I don't think anyone except you knows. Otherwise they would be here by now."

"I won't tell," he said grimly. She smiled wanly.

"Are you sure you don't want to while away some time?" she asked, her hand rising to the buttons of her gown furtively. "You have to wait until the cops are finished pretending they are helping."

"Now that you mention it," he reminded, turning

towards her. "You can't go out either – you have a boot print from that *nedonosok* on your leg."

"You're right," colour drained from her face. "Oh hell, I have to make some calls."

"In that case," he told her. "How about you do some work for me?"

"Didn't I just offer?"

"No, not like that," he replied. "I need some information."

"Yes," she said. "If I can. What do you want?"

"I need to find some officers who served in my corps fifteen years ago."

"Fifteen years?" she smiled bleakly. "How old were you?"

"Never mind," he retorted irritably. "Can you help me or not?"

She thought for a while.

"I know someone," she said slowly. "I think he could do that. He is a friend, he'll help."

"Can I trust him to keep quiet?" asked Mironov.

"Most definitely," she replied with a chuckle. "He had some problems with the FSB. If he causes any more, they will get very nasty. He won't want to attract their attention."

She put her hands to her temples, thinking.

"All right," she said. "Give me a few days. Then we could call him safely."

"Good," replied Mironov. "I might just get some more sleep."

She nodded and reached for the telephone.

***

He awoke with a leaden taste in the mouth, his body stiff and sore. It was now late in the afternoon, the sky darkening with storm clouds that seemed to have come from nowhere.

He stretched and walked into the kitchen. Nina nearly ran to meet him from the lounge. Her leg now appeared to be healed.

"Are you all right?" she asked.

"Yes," he replied with a frown. "Why?"

"You slept for two days," she said. "How do you feel?"

"Could do with a little more," he admitted.

"Is there some weird reason for the way you are?" she asked with suspicion. He shrugged at the question.

"Weird is a word you people have lost the right to use," he replied, gesturing to the window. "Armed mayhem on the streets of Moscow, so-called patriots worshipping Stalin and Hitler, good women selling their bodies – no, compared to all that mine is quite a mundane story."

"And what might that be?" she asked acidly.

"Oh, just coming back from the dead," he replied

with a terse smile.

"That is unusual," she acknowledged with a wry expression. "Nowadays, traffic is mostly in the opposite direction."

He searched her face for any signs of surprise, but only saw irony.

"All right," he pronounced. "Don't ask any questions – the less you know, the fewer headaches you will have."

"Oh, headaches," she said lightly. "There are many headaches in Moscow. Headaches are nothing new."

"The headaches I cause are nine millimetres in diameter," he replied. "The less you have to do with me, the better."

"I've called my friend," she said, shrugging her shoulders. "He will be here tonight with his machine."

He nodded and helped himself to a piece of bread.

"Would you like some dinner?" asked Nina.

"No, this is fine," he replied, chewing on the hard rye.

She shrugged her shoulders and left him in the kitchen alone.

Later he took a shower for the first time in many days, rubbing his body under very hot water to work the knots out of tired muscles.

He noticed it when he emerged from the shower to rub his skin dry with a rough towel. He stared for a long time, then finished drying himself and dressed, eyes burning with triumphant fire.

Nina's friend arrived at six, a young man with a heavy stubble and thick glasses. His lank dark hair was long and greasy, and the upper lip was stained orange with tobacco.

He introduced himself as Andrei and shook hands with Mironov, Andrei's effeminate, slender fingers disappearing inside the shovel-like palm.

Andrei carried with him a small pouch that resembled a briefcase worn on a strap over the shoulder. He carefully set it down on the sofa as Nina poured him a generous serve of vodka. Mironov sat opposite him at the dinner table.

"So what are you looking for, Comrade Major?" asked Andrei deferentially.

"I have four names," said Mironov. "All men who served in my sector during the Afghan war. I need to know their current whereabouts, dead or alive."

He handed over a piece of paper he took from the conductor on the train. It contained a list in Mironov's angular handwriting, compiled over the last hundred kilometres of snow-bound expanse before Moscow.

"Okay," said Andrei. "This should not be hard."

"Can you do this in a week?" asked Mironov.

"I don't think this should be a problem," repeated Andrei.

He opened the case he brought with him and removed the most compact computer Mironov ever saw. He connected it by cable to a mobile telephone and turned it on.

What followed was entirely incomprehensible to Mironov. He ceased paying attention after the first fifteen minutes, choosing to stand at the window. Forehead pressed to the cold glass pane, he admired the ocean of dim lights that was a Moscow night in late November.

Suddenly he heard Andrei's voice and turned around.

"Write this down, Major," said Andrei.

Mironov hurriedly took the pen Nina proffered him and scrawled on the back of his hand. There were three addresses in Moscow and one in Yaroslavl, a small historic city not far from Moscow. Nina found him some paper, and he sat down to rewrite the information properly.

"That's it," affirmed Andrei triumphantly. He typed a few instructions and closed his computer, packing it into the bag.

"Thank you," said Mironov in amazement. "Was it safe?"

"Yes," replied Andrei. "Completely. I've just tapped into a few army databases anonymously. They couldn't trace this in a million years."

"You just did what?"

"Oh, they were only low-level rubbish," shrugged Andrei. "Pension funds, decoration lists, that kind of thing. It's not like I stole missile codes."

Mironov nodded suspiciously.

"I better get going," said Andrei with a slight edge to his voice. "It's getting late."

"Thank you," Mironov told him. They shook hands, and Andrei left hurriedly.

"He is a good kid," said Nina with a chuckle as she shut the door. "Really clever with computers. Got himself into trouble a few years ago – he transferred a million dollars from a French bank to Greenpeace. The French tracked him all the way here."

"So what happened?" asked Mironov with genuine curiosity.

"He was lucky," replied Nina. "The bank people were desperate to know how he did it, so they persuaded our authorities to leave him alone if he told them."

"How do you know him?" asked Mironov.

"He used to live next door to my family," said Nina. "Before I got married and came here."

"Married?" asked Mironov, his eyebrows rising.

Nina nodded sadly.

"Helicopter pilot," she said. "Rather not talk about him."

"I am sorry," retreated Mironov grimly.

She nodded again.

"It was a long time ago," she said, dropping her

head onto her chin for a brief moment. Then she looked up at Mironov.

"What will you do now?" she asked.

"I need to get to Yaroslavl," he replied. "Know anyone with a car?"

She chuckled and nodded.

"Get some more sleep," she said. "I'll ring someone to pick you up at first light tomorrow, but it'll cost you."

"Wake me up when ready," he commanded and went to bed.

***

His order was fulfilled early next morning. Pale sunshine drifting into the window, he rubbed his eyes and padded to the bathroom.

When he emerged, Nina was ready with three slices of black bread and a carafe of water. He ate whilst she explained about Yaroslavl.

The road was blocked for an entire week by bandits, who simply stopped buses and cars and robbed their occupants at gunpoint. They were not, apparently, very numerous, but neither the army nor the police were prepared to guarantee safety to those travelling there. So they simply closed the highway, much used by tourist buses, at both ends to avoid any international incidents.

Getting around this blockade would be child's play in the summer, but two meters of snow made it a less trivial exercise. However, Nina knew some people whose business, apparently, was to get their merchandise into Yaroslavl without fail, and they quickly set up an alternative route through back roads. They weren't overly interested in taking Mironov's money, so long as he took part in any actions of self-defence which may be required.

Mironov nodded, bemused. He noticed that his consent was not sought to make this arrangement, nor was he asked for such consent now. He took both the Makarov and the thug's machine pistol, strapping the latter to his body under the leather coat.

Nina kept watching out of the window, then sent him outside to meet Vasily, a nondescript man in a short coat, *valenki* felt boots and a fur *shapka* on his bald head, who waited for him next to a battered Volga of 1960's vintage. Two more men waited inside the ancient vehicle.

They shook hands and made introductions. Vasily pointed to the front seat, and they took off, Mironov instantly becoming aware that the car's vintage engine was replaced by something large and powerful.

Speeding through the empty morning streets, Vasily asked if he was armed. Mironov pulled open his leather coat and showed him.

Vasily nodded, and they went over the cover story. There was virtually no police to be found, he explained, but you never know if a patrol might lose its way.

The boot was apparently full of second-hand electronic goods they bought on the flea market. They were now on the way back to their village, Razdeevo, just this side of the Yaroslavl blockade. Mironov was a nephew, who breezed in to spend the New Year with his sister's family from....?

"Taman'," replied Mironov, citing his last prewar post.

"Wonderful place," nodded Vasily with enthusiasm.

They stopped at an intersection, and Mironov watched with amazement as a group of beggars tried to make their way to the car but stopped dead at Vasily's forceful gesture. As they waited for the light to change Mironov saw two men and a woman in dark military-style dress uniforms approach the beggars.

"Who are the *mundiri*?" he asked, referring to the uniforms.

"*Armia Spasenia*," chuckled Vasily.

Mironov looked at him in wonderment.

"American Christians," said Vasily, rotating his finger around his temple to indicate insanity. "Helping the poor, pissing in the ocean, you know?"

Mironov nodded grimly as the lights changed, and the vehicle took off.

"I've been away a very long time," he replied to the probing looks from the men in the back seat.

"Aha," nodded one of them. "Must have been a few years."

"Quite a few," confirmed Mironov curtly.

"Where were you stationed?" asked the other.

"First *Afgan*, then... places," said Mironov.

All conversation ceased, cut by the lifetime's ingrained fear of even appearing to solicit classified information.

They were on the intercity highway, travelling fast along the steel-reinforced concrete with numerous potholes. It was dry enough because of its traffic, but now Vasily drove in the cautious manner of a man who wants to avoid attention. The rest of the landscape was shrouded in dense snow.

Mironov looked ahead sombrely, his experienced eyes scanning the landscape for any discontinuity of contour. Vasily noticed this after a while and patted him on the shoulder.

"Not here," he said with a small smile. "The bad part is when we leave the road."

Outside the city the traffic more or less ceased apart from occasional trucks and military vehicles. An hour into the trip Vasily extracted a mobile phone from the pocket and called someone. He appeared to receive a situation report, nodded and hung up without saying a word.

A short time after that one-sided conversation Vasily pulled the car off the highway and turned into a snow-bound lane. It was heavily used, the snow on it compacted and navigable, but he slowed right down all the same.

They drove a little more than a kilometre off the main highway when a small tracked utility vehicle emerged from the nearby forest and met them alongside the road.

Two men from the back seat silently unloaded boxes with what appeared to be television sets out of the boot and carried them over to the utility. Vasily turned around and drove away, leaving Mironov alone with the three men. The driver stayed inside the cabin.

They climbed into the tray, and the vehicle rumbled off. A sweet pain chilled Mironov's stomach – the engine note was just like that of his tank.

They made themselves as comfortable as possible, a mild cross-wind still forgiving to bare faces. The vehicle rumbled off into the forest down what appeared to be a snow-bound track.

One of the men pulled out a small bottle of vodka and initiated *na troih*, an eternally Russian ritual that consists of dividing a half-litre of sacred fluid into three precisely even portions, using no instrumentation whatsoever. Whoever exceeds his share is beaten up, unless he happens to be the last – in which case it is his right to benefit from his comrades' caution.

Mironov hesitated slightly – drinking whilst in charge of a weapon was a new experience he did not crave. But the trip promised to be very, very cold without even a crude tarpaulin to cover the passengers.

He winced as he poured the last portion down his throat. The spirit hit him fast, inflaming his cheeks and burning the insides. He looked around the tray and dropped the bottle into a wooden crate in the corner.

"Throw it away," suggested one of the men.

"Bad to leave traces," replied Mironov mildly. The other two nodded in acknowledgement of this wisdom.

The ritual concluded, the men unbuttoned their coats and extracted their weapons. Both carried a *Malysh*, a smaller version of the ubiquitous AK-47.

Mironov tensed slightly, but then relaxed as guns were checked and pointed overboard. He removed the machine pistol and prepared to protect his side.

Carried forward by a rumbling diesel, he lay in

the tray, mind whirling. He was travelling across a Russian countryside in the closing years of the twentieth century with what was almost certainly a large amount of drugs. Not only that, but he was helping to protect that load from individuals even more criminal than his companions, and his finely honed military skills would be the only thing that would protect his life if he met such people.

Mironov grew up in the golden years of the Soviet Union when open resistance to the regime was, with some justification, regarded as an act of insanity. The present reality worse than bad fiction – Mironov had no choice but to draw that conclusion.

He had read about lawless times in the aftermath of the Russian Revolution and always found descriptions of that far-off mayhem improbable, propaganda concocted to blacken the counter-revolutionaries. Now he felt that if anything, those Civil War stories were probably toned down.

None of it, however, stopped him from revelling in the timeless beauty of a Russian forest encased in virgin snow, a myriad of silhouettes in a frozen dance of still perfection. Four colours – white of the snow, black and green of the trees and a delicate blue of the sky – resonated in his chest, a Russian's primal joy at returning to his ethereally beautiful land from a treeless and waterless landscape densely sown with death and decay.

The forest eventually ended. Far from embracing his relatives in the village of Razdeevo, Mironov found himself skirting it by a wide margin. They hugged the edge where what looked like a cultivated field met forest, the driver gunning the engine over that open expanse.

"Vipers' nest!" spat one of Mironov's companions, waving at the village. "We broke down there last week – the way they looked at us, I thought we'd get our throats cut for sure – thank God Vasily arrived with the boys."

Mironov nodded, expecting this fact to elicit amazement, but his ability to be amazed was becoming numbed with each new assault on that sensibility.

They were back in the forest, dropping speed to accommodate the winding track. The wind now died down, and Mironov began to genuinely enjoy the trip.

The ambush site was chosen well, situated where the track passed through a narrow ravine. The steep sides were densely covered with fir trees and could have provided superb cover for an entire regiment.

Yet the attackers made poor use of that advantage, arranging most of their gunmen on one side only. That told Mironov, as he sought cover in the flimsy tray, that the enemy was neither experienced nor disciplined, the riflemen too lazy to cross the path and climb the opposite hill to prepare a proper trap.

The bad news was that his companions did not perform under fire either. One appeared to have collapsed with a bad shoulder wound, losing his weapon overboard. The other stood on his knees, escaping a hail of bullets through nothing more than miracle. He fired back ineffectually, most of his ammunition expended with no impact on the attackers. Mironov reached over and restrained him by lowering his barrel. Then he took hold of the man's sleeve and forced him down to shelter inside the tray.

The driver was alive and apparently well, possibly owing to the reluctance of attackers to fire at the nearby fuel tank. The engine compartment was dented by numerous rounds, but thick Soviet-era sheet metal held well. The radiator grille was protected by a Venetian blind-like arrangement fitted to Russian vehicles to keep engines warm during extremely low temperatures, and this rude construction proved strong enough to stop stray bullets.

The utility kept moving in deeper snow, managing to burst through a half-hearted barricade of young firs, piled up a little distance past the ambush. The idea, surmised Mironov, was to drive them from the stuck vehicle once ammunition ran out, but the barricade proved too flimsy. The barricade was good news – it was unlikely that the enemy would have a contingency plan in case they broke through.

The pursuit party emerged from behind clumps of trees in two snowmobiles and screamed towards them from both sides.

Mironov signalled to his companion to move to the rear of the tray, and they crawled, keeping their heads down as an occasional bullet whistled above them to ricochet off the back of the cabin.

Listening for the sound of approaching engines, Mironov pulled at the slide of his machine pistol. He placed the barrel on the edge of the tray, and his companion did likewise.

Mironov held up his hand in a restraining gesture, rocking the palm to indicate increasing readiness as the drone of snowmobiles approached. He didn't like the wild look in the man's eyes, his officer's instinct noted, but this was not the time to chastise subordinates.

With the sound of the snowmobiles nearly upon them, he suddenly cocked his wrist to angle the barrel over the tray's edge and sprayed bullets at the oncoming vehicles. Out of the corner of his eye he noted his companion mimicking his action correctly.

The manoeuvre had the desired effect. One snowmobile exploded in a ball of flame, the other veered sharply into deep snow and hit some immovable object, throwing both of its occupants hard over the handlebars.

The occasional bullet still whistled over their heads as they sped off, but it was clear that the assault was over. Soon the track made a thankful hard turn that concealed them from attackers, and Mironov exhaled a deep breath of relief.

They unbuttoned the coat of the wounded man, who was now unconscious. His companion contrived to tie a rag from the wooden crate around the wound pulsing with hot, sticky blood. Mironov stuffed the empty vodka bottle into the sleeve to press the rag to the wound harder, and they re-buttoned the ruined coat tight over that improvisation.

The other man rose to his feet and walked over to the cabin. He used the butt of his assault rifle to knock on the small window in the rear wall, succeeding in attracting the driver's attention. He held up his bloody hand and pointed at the wounded man urgently.

Blue smoke belched from the vertical exhaust stack as the accelerator was pressed to the floor. The machine increased speed reluctantly but was moving respectably fast as they exited the forest, running across another wheat field covered with snow. Mironov watched the driver raise someone on the mobile phone, as he looked back at the unconscious man with horror.

In less than an hour they made it to another country lane whose traffic compressed the snow into a hard surface. The driver slowed to navigate the drop into the lane, then pointed the machine along the road and gathered speed.

Shortly afterwards they were met by a convoy of vehicles plentifully crewed with armed men. The wounded gunman was carried into the back of a gleaming Land Cruiser, which immediately reversed and sped off into the distance.

The other vehicles accompanied them to a small cluster of houses, where the cargo was unloaded, and Mironov was taken to board another old Volga, to share the back seat with his new comrade in arms, who shakily thanked him for saving their lives.

The convoy took off down the snow-bound lane, the man seated in the front seat turning to toss them a bottle of vodka. Both drank lustily and returned the bottle half-full.

The man in the front did not imbibe, but he nodded at them with the respect accorded to veterans of a recent firefight by men under arms.

"You hurt?" he asked briskly. Both shook their heads.

"Load up," he said, passing them a box of ammunition. "They could catch up with us."

"What about the driver?" asked Mironov.

"Oh, don't worry about him," said Rudik. "He has a full squad back at that farm. With their machine guns he is safe. If anything happens at all, those bastards will come after us."

Mironov nodded and examined his machine pistol's magazine. He was nearly out, and his were 9mm pistol rounds. The man at the front reached under his seat and handed him a box of those, which Mironov half-used to reload, pocketing the rest.

There was no further trouble. They made it to the main highway, their four-hour trip having bypassed a hundred kilometres of the road blocked with varying success by both bandits and authorities.

The light began to recede as they reached Yaroslavl, a small historic town filled with churches and, normally, tourist buses. It was now grimly quiet, the convoy speeding unimpeded down the wide streets.

"Where do you need to go?" asked the driver. Mironov recited the address.

"It's not far," said the driver. "Is this someone we know?"

The others thought and shook their heads.

"Good," replied the driver. "But don't make too much noise. We have a good thing going with the cops, and we told them there won't be any trouble inside the city, okay?"

"There will be no noise whatsoever," said Mironov grimly. "Listen – don't drop me at that address. Just drive past it and point it out to me, then drop me off about a kilometre further down."

The driver chuckled briefly.

"*Osnaz*?" he asked quietly, looking at Mironov in the rear view mirror.

"No," replied Mironov firmly. *Osnaz*, or particular purpose units, were KGB. His special purpose force, *spetznaz*, was military. There was fierce rivalry between these elite units.

"Sure," the driver chuckled again. "You must have served in the medical corps."

"No," declared Mironov without a change in tone.

"Whatever," said the driver. "Never mind – we

are grateful. When and where do you want to be picked up?"

"Same time tomorrow," replied Mironov. "Make it somewhere in the centre of town."

"Main square," announced the driver without hesitation. "The *shashlyk* kiosk, between two and three in the afternoon. If you aren't there, we don't know who you are."

"Fine," Mironov told him.

They turned the corner and slowed down slightly.

"Look left," said the driver. "Fourth house, it's the one painted yellow."

Mironov's eyes slid over a three-storey apartment building, whose façade was perforated by a single arched entrance. It was indeed painted yellow, but that blessed event must have taken place before the Bolshevik takeover, when the once-luxurious building was relatively new.

They turned right at the next corner and continued along the street. The driver picked a spot between two large factories, the street being flanked by tall brick fences on both sides. If they were being observed, it wasn't obvious.

"Tomorrow," repeated the driver. "Remember,

between fourteen and fifteen hundred, *shashlyk* kiosk, main square."

Mironov nodded once and got out. As soon as he shut the door the car took off, accelerating sharply once he was out of reach of spraying snow. The rest of the convoy sped past him, leaving him entirely alone.

He walked back to the apartment block in fading light, the snow completely muffling the sound of his steps. There was very little traffic on a dull weeknight, and he felt very noticeable in the empty street.

When he turned the corner he spotted his first problem. A large doorman with an ancient revolver on a Sam Browne belt was pacing in the arched driveway. Framed by an untidy beard, his large face was relaxed and bored, but he moved with long, elastic strides that betrayed strength and fitness at variance with a yokel appearance.

Mironov didn't alter his stride as he walked past. He kept on walking to the distant supermarket where three young men slouched next to the wall, collars of their cheap parkas upturned to keep out the gathering cold.

Mironov walked up to them and signalled for them to follow him inside, his hand showing them a fifty-dollar bill. Their expressions of languid boredom immediately tightened with interest.

They followed him into a supermarket aisle where he randomly selected a few bottles of imported beer. They went outside and stood next to a garbage container which concealed their gathering from the doorman.

"Simple deal," proclaimed Mironov, distributing the beer.

He noted the Lenin badges which all three wore on their lapels. Communism must be eternal, he thought with rare amusement. Like inherent human idiocy.

"Walk down to the yellow house where that bloated fascist guards the driveway and start drinking outside. When you run dry, smash the bottles on his wall and start a fight. If you can get him to come out of the driveway and look the other way for a minute, you will find this American money tucked in the snowdrift on the other side of the archway. Interested?"

"What are you going to do?" asked one of the boys, a tall blond lad with shoulders already starting to bulge with muscle.

"I need to serve some documents on one of the rich criminals who live inside," said Mironov. "But the law says that they don't have to let me in. If I happen to a find a way inside, that's my fortune."

"What's he done?" asked another boy, whose freckled face was deformed by a large scar running across his left cheek.

"Can't say," replied Mironov.

The deal was struck, and three miscreants set out to amble along the street, drinking their beer. Mironov followed them at a discrete distance.

They affected a reprehensible performance, spraying the street with broken glass and breaking into a noisy fight with much abuse and other noises. It took careful observation to see that their energetic antics were not, in fact, leaving bruises on fellow Leninists.

Their patron saint wasn't like that at all, thought Mironov. Lenin spent most of his energy on slandering, back-stabbing and executing his fellow revolutionaries, paying only modest attention to the proletarian struggle against oppressors.

In fact the runt had little choice, hand-fed as he was in millionaires' Zurich by German intelligence, under the intent gaze of bourgeois authorities. The Swiss stood ready to pounce at the slightest hint of trouble, but meanwhile they ensured that the exiled champion of workers and peasants had his fill of all luxuries on offer. When the time was finally ripe,

Lenin was trucked into the void left by the Czar's abdication in a German armoured train, and that train arrived precisely on schedule.

Lenins's comrades, on the other hand, supplied him with nothing but hot air. Any genius of his calibre would conclude that he was better off doing amicable deals with the enemies of world revolution and applying the fury of the oppressed to his Marxist brethren instead.

After less than a minute the guard marched out into the street, his right hand close to the holster at his side. He shouted with authority and dispensed a few well-aimed kicks – which the boys allowed to land. They then held up their hands and gathered themselves up, giving the guard a respectfully wide berth.

He glared at them fiercely until they moved away. In near-darkness he failed to see one of them lean towards a snowdrift and extract something from the snow.

Mironov completed the dash inside the arched driveway and casually turned the corner into the yard as if he had strolled in from the street. The apartment block was built in classic Russian style – a quadrangle enclosing an inner courtyard, kitchen windows overlooking it like machine gun embrasures. Mironov strode through the courtyard, squinting at the numbers above doorways.

He eventually found the right stairwell and ascended to the second floor noiselessly. He found the door and stopped in front of it, listening for any noise on the stairs.

There was none. He leaned to press his ear to the solid wood and stayed there, listening for any sounds inside the apartment.

There weren't any. Mironov padded to the next landing and positioned himself out of sight. He checked the Makarov and waited motionlessly.

An hour later a man descended from the floor above with a large German shepherd. When they came past Mironov pressed a gloved fist to his left ear and pushed his head into a corner, pretending to be engrossed in a conversation on a mobile phone. He nodded enthusiastically and periodically mumbled his assent into his hand until the man with his dog emerged from the landing into the yard.

He sat still for another hour. The man and the dog returned, and Mironov raced up to the the top floor where he waited until he heard them enter their apartment. He then padded back down the stairs and resumed his wait.

Close to midnight he was finally rewarded – a tall man in an elegant Burberry and a sable fur hat struggled up the stairs, set down a heavy suitcase and fumbled with keys. After operating two locks he reached inside and deactivated the alarm on the pad near the door.

Concentrating on these actions in near-darkness prevented him from seeing a shadow that soundlessly whirled down the banister and flew at him from behind. He was smashed in the back of his head with a pistol butt, the momentum of the assailant lifting both off their feet. He slammed into the doorway heavily and was unconscious by the time he hit the floor.

When he came to he was amazed to find himself expertly tied to a heavy armchair with fragments of the clothesline from his balcony. His elegant lounge appeared undisturbed, except for the case that was now open on the floor. It was full of mobile phones.

His attacker made himself very comfortable indeed. He sat opposite, coat off and muscular body radiating the scent of cheap soap. He wore a leather glove on the right hand, and a pistol was tucked into his pants.

"Captain Mashkin," the intruder declared coldly. "How good to resume our acquaintance."

"What is this about?" stammered Mashkin with bewilderment.

"Let's see if you can remember," the visitor stood up and towered over him. "It was a rather important occasion for me, so it would truly wound me if you don't recall it."

Mashkin nodded hastily.

"A cold morning in a Panshir valley," began the intruder. "You are the duty captain in base MR-1210."

"Seven days a week for six months," confirmed Mashkin quickly.

"Very well. On one particular morning you ordered a major in charge of a motorized special operations unit to turn back into a sector where he had just conducted an operation."

Mashkin thought hard.

"The reason why you might recall that occasion is that the order was as good as a death sentence," hissed the intruder, hatred smouldering through his sarcastic demeanour. "That officer just reported his position and explained that he shot up a weapons convoy. Sending him back through that sector on a nonsensical mission was plain murder."

"I do remember this," whispered Mashkin, shaking his head in disbelief.

"Excellent," replied the visitor, his mouth tightening with contempt. "Then you will enlighten me as to why you had expended their lives."

He sat down at his chair and folded his hands into his lap in expectation.

"I am sorry," whispered Mashkin. "I don't know. I just did as they ordered."

"A model officer," nodded the visitor approvingly. "They would adore you at Nuremberg. However, you will find me more exacting."

A series of blows rained on Mashkin's neatly groomed face, pulping his lips and flattening his nose. He passed out after a hard punch loosened his front teeth.

He came awake some time later, cold water dripping down his face. He peeled open his swollen eyelids in time to see his tormentor place the bucket on the floor and turn towards him.

"Ah," proclaimed Mironov hatefully. "Welcome back. I've planned a long entertainment program designed to improve your memory, and I wouldn't care for you to miss any of it."

"I still don't understand," breathed Mashkin, barely moving the torn lips encrusted with blood.

"I am not going to repeat anything," replied the visitor. "Except the punches."

"Please," whispered Mashkin. "I really don't know why they ordered me to do it. You can kill me, but I can't tell you anything I don't know."

"All right then," agreed the intruder, taking out his pistol casually. He removed the clip, checked that it was full, slapping it back into the butt. His hand whipped across and operated the slide with frightening speed, and Mashkin felt the barrel pressed to his forehead. He shuddered involuntarily.

"Where do you want it, rear echelon rodent?" asked Mironov coldly. The barrel of the pistol started sliding down Mashkin's face, throat, chest, then stomach – stopping just above the groin. He moaned in horror.

"Don't worry," added Mironov, a chilling smile creasing his mask of hatred. "If you choose the first bullet badly, I have many more to spare."

The barrel pressed tighter into Mashkin's belt line.

"Look," said Mashkin, trying to sound calm despite the chattering of his remaining teeth. "All I know is this. Your commander reports your coordinates, I post them on the board, then Berezov's adjutant runs out and screams at me."

"Ah, your memory is recovering," suggested Mironov mockingly, easing the pressure of the barrel by a fraction.

"What is this column doing in that valley, he screams," continued Mashkin in a desperate effort to buy time. "I merely shrug my shoulders; I have just taken over the post. Then Colonel Golubkov overhears the conversation and says to the adjutant, look, those troops are a roving *spetznaz* patrol. They can go there, they can go here, and they can go up your baby arse if they so wanted."

"Proceed."

"The adjutant runs out, and I know he ran to speak to the general who is in the showers or some such. Then the adjutant marches back and announces the new orders."

"And?"

"Well," Mashkin hesitated. "I get on the radio and tell your commanding officer."

"You are a model of your kind," commented Mironov viciously. "Anything else?"

"Your commanding officer questioned the orders," Mashkin continued . "So I verified them. I made the adjutant run back and ask again."

"Were they confirmed?"

"They were. Berezov was pretty angry to be

asked again, and he ordered that I convey this as well. Which I did."

"Why did the commander question the orders?" asked Mironov evenly.

"He said they would get all of your men killed," Mashkin answered without hesitation.

"Now," said Mironov, pressing the gun into Mashkin's stomach. "Did that bother you?"

"No," replied Mashkin with a note of defiance.

"Why is that?" inquired Mironov with genuine curiosity.

"They all said that," replied Mashkin. "All who went out on those missions."

"I see," said Mironov, nodding in appraisal. "And did they all die?"

"They did, mostly," replied Mashkin earnestly.

"Do you know what happened to that column?"

"Yes," Mashkin lowered his gaze away from him. "Two tanks escaped with full crew, the rest were all killed. The commanding officer kept on firing from a burning tank to cover their escape. He was awarded the Order of Lenin posthumously.

There was a funeral for him – I never saw such grief as amongst his surviving men."

Mironov watched in amazement as tears poured down Mashkin's face.

"Fuck it," whispered Mashkin, his voice trembling. "Fuck it dead, I am tired of living with all those memories. Shoot me and get it over with. Who are you, anyway?"

"I am that commander," replied Mironov. He thumbed the safety catch and replaced the pistol behind his belt.

"No, damn it!" countered Mashkin, voice rising in annoyance. "Whoever you are, you are not that man. He must have died horribly."

"Not too bad," said Mironov. "Blown to dust in one instant."

"So you can't be he," explained Mashkin placatingly, now convinced that he was dealing with a madman.

"But I am," replied Mironov, extracting his military passport from the coat on the nearby chair to splay it open in front of his prisoner.

Mashkin studied the photograph, and his blood-shot eyes bored into Mironov.

"This has to be a mistake," he said shakily.

"No, Comrade," said Mironov. "No mistake. I died in that tank, and now I am here."

"How can that be?" asked Mashkin indignantly.

"In truth, Comrade, I have no idea. Yet that is what appears to have happened," replied Mironov dreamily. "However, it seems appropriate that if a man dies and leaves behind such outrage, he may be rejected by his very grave. Much as he wishes to stay dead, he should return to put things right, especially if he is so eminently qualified for that mission."

"Very pretty," commented Mashkin tartly. "But if that were to be, no dead would find rest in Russia."

"That may yet transpire," replied Mironov evenly. "Now, my final question. I understand you don't know why Berezov did this for a fact, but were there rumours?"

"For what they were worth," admitted Mashkin.

"Such as?"

"Heroin, said the wind."

"What?!!"

"Oh yes, Comrade," replied Mashkin grimly. "It was the beginning of the heroin problem in Russia. The fucking CIA taught *Duhi* to grow poppies to pay for their weapons. Rumour was, Berezov was way ahead of his time. He would have traded stolen weapon consignments for drugs and imported heroin into Soviet Union on military transports. I don't know this for a fact, but it makes sense. He is now a very powerful man."

"What did my unit have to do with his grubby deals?" asked Mironov.

"I believe you unexpectedly turned up in the wrong sector and might have been headed towards his men," Mashkin answered. "I don't know, it's just my suspicion that you were probably turned around and sent to your deaths to prevent you seeing something."

Mironov nodded, assessing this information. His face was a dark thundercloud.

"All right," he said slowly. "Here's the deal. If you remember the name of the adjutant, I'll let you live."

It's not much of an incentive," replied Mashkin sourly. "But I am certain his name was Nikolayev. Yes. Igor Nikolayev."

"Rank?"

"Captain, like myself. We joked behind his back that it was just as well he was a captain in the infantry. Were he a captain in charge of ship, it would sink before leaving port."

"Very well. I will leave you now – after all, you are not the man that gave the order. You and I deserve to die for the sickening things we've done, Captain Mashkin. We all belong on the gallows we constructed in Nuremberg. But there isn't enough rope to punish all the guilty, and there will be no Nurembergs in Russia. So I see no reason to single you out."

"Untie me then," said Mashkin. "This is not pleasant."

"Oh," Mironov whirled around in mock surprise. "Would you like a gun as well?"

"Fuck off."

"I'll call the cops a little later and tell them where you are," said Mironov. He walked over to the suitcase and helped himself to a small black phone, holding it with awe. "Say, how does this wonder work anyway?"

"Turn it on at the side," replied Mashkin. "Punch in the code written on the back, then press the 'Send' button."

"Done."

"Now just dial your number and press 'Send'. When you are finished, press 'Send' again."

"Impressive," said Mironov. "I'll leave you now."
He dressed and walked towards the door, turning at the threshold.

"One more thing," he added. "Go see this Nikolayev. Give him and his friends a message from me."

"What's that?" asked Mashkin. He lay back in the armchair, his eyelids beginning to swell shut.

"Tell them about me," replied Mironov slowly. "Tell them death will come for them soon. They can try to run or they can fight if they like – it won't make any difference. I am on the way."

"You and what army?" asked Mashkin acidly, opening his eyes. "They are very well protected. These are men who expect a fight to the death every minute of every day."

Mironov chuckled and looked at Mashkin coldly, hand poised on the door handle.

"Then they are in luck," he affirmed quietly. "Their wait is nearly over."

He stepped out, taking care to pull the door shut until the locks engaged. Mashkin spat out a weak curse and leaned back into his chair. A trickle of urine snaked down the leather chair to the parquet floor.

***

Mironov strolled around the *shashlyk* kiosk twice before he detected a spot where he could wait inconspicuously. He looked at his watch and observed the traffic in the square.

There were a lot of beggars who first tried to zero on him. One vicious flash of his eyes sent them scurrying away, but as he settled down to wait, his gaze was drawn to their multitude – old men and women of all ages, some with small children.

Wearing thin leather gloves Mironov wiped the phone on his shirt. Then he used it to call the local militia, stating that a victim of an attempted burglary is tied up at Mashkin's address. He switched it off and slid out the battery for good measure.

The designated time had nearly expired when the Volga turned up with the same three men. Mironov strolled out into the square as they approached, only heading towards them at the last moment. As they opened the door he tossed Mashkin's phone to a woman with a vacant-eyed small child, who stood in the snow beside a begging bowl.

"So you made it," pronounced the driver genially. "Any trouble?"

"Nil," replied Mironov. The other man waited for more details, but none came.

"Excellent," the driver said at length. "I suppose you want to go back to Moscow now."

"As soon as possible," Mironov answered neutrally.

"Too bad," said the driver wistfully. "We could always use a good man."

"Maybe later," suggested Mironov. "I am on assignment now."

"Lucrative?" asked one of the men in the back seat.

"Not as such," replied Mironov.

"Could we maybe pay you to quit?" asked the man.

"No," replied Mironov, shaking his head in amazement. "It's personal."

"Oh," said the man. "When you finish, perhaps. I have no doubt you will survive whatever you are planning."

Mironov nodded in contemplation. It was getting dark, the car speeding through outskirts of town towards the highway.

***

Mironov stepped off the metro train and rode the upward escalator outside. He crossed the square in front of the station's neoclassical façade and pulled out a new phone he had purchased earlier that day.

He checked his list and dialled a number from the top entry, pressing the phone buttons with what could pass for a fear of electrocution.

Mironov pressed the device to his ear and relaxed, hearing familiar noises on the line.

"What?" asked a harsh female voice abruptly.

"I need to speak to Sergei Trofimovich," said Mironov in a robotic, even tone.

"Who's this?" demanded the woman, her manner now downright hostile.

"Is that you, Anna Nikolayevna?" said Mironov, his voice trembling slightly. He recognized her timbre, cracked with the passage of years, yet still unmistakably hers.

"Sure. Who are you, though?" she replied without a change of tone.

"Mironov," he whispered, his voice starting to break with emotion. "This is Viktor Mironov."

"What kind of blasphemy is this?" shrilled the

woman angrily. "Whoever you are, have you no respect, Satan spawn?"

"Anna Nikolayevna," announced Mironov, wiping his eyes. "I am back among the living."

"Major Mironov? Vitya?..." she repeated mechanically, at last recognizing his voice. "Vitya… My husband always said you would hammer your way out of any hell. Is this really you?"

"It is, dear lady," replied Mironov. "It is. Where is he?"

"Wait," she sobbed. "I will fetch him."

She shouted something with her hand over the receiver, then there were muffled voices, and Sergeant Grishin, now long retired from the elite Guards, came on the line.

"Major," he said slowly. "Is it true?"

"I am here," answered Mironov. "In the flesh."

"I must see you."

"I am coming over in half-an-hour."

"Yes."

Mironov pressed the off button a few times and listened to ensure that the phone stopped transmitting. He slid it into a pocket and began to walk.

Just on twenty minutes later he crossed a series of wide streets that separated concrete lumps of high rise apartments, their façades peeling and meagre, landscaping around them strewn with garbage. He found the building he needed and thumbed the phone again, telling Grishin that he was outside.

A few minutes later the reinforced steel door of the block across the road was flung open, and Grishin rushed out with his wife – a tall man with ramrod bearing running through the snow in flimsy slippers.

He ran up to Mironov and stopped a short distance away, staring intensely. Grishin still had an immensely powerful frame, but his hair was now mostly white, face weathered and wrinkled. The long, straight nose still protruded over a thinner face with handlebar moustache, and his features were creased in consternation.

"This cannot be," he said under his breath. Then he embraced his commanding officer, and both streamed bitter tears. Anna Nikolayevna, a short, dumpy woman with a kind face topped by a home-cut mop of grey hair, safed the pistol she held under her apron and shook her head in disbelief.

"Were you captured?" asked Grishin.

Mironov shook his head curtly.

"Paratroops?" asked Grishin. "Did they rescue you after we escaped?"

"No," said Mironov evenly. "I was left by myself, fired a pistol into the primer of a phosphorus round, killed most of the *Duhi* and got blown to dust myself. Then a week ago I woke up on a train as it was pulling into Novosibirsky *vokzal*. Now you know all I know."

Grishin's wife crossed herself rapidly.

"Everyone inside," she ordered. They trudged back through unkempt snow into the apartment block and caught a relatively clean lift with zinc, morgue-like walls, to the top floor.

Inside the apartment Grishin held out his hand for Mironov's coat and nodded at the sight of his weapons. Anna Nikolayevna produced a bottle of frozen vodka and some snacks that provide the aesthetic angle of social intoxication, that celebrated cornerstone of Russian life.

They drank and tossed pieces of pickled cucumber into their mouths. Mironov winced from the burn and placed his hand over his glass as the bottle made the second round with no delay whatsoever. Anna Nikolayevna smoothly bypassed him, refilling the remaining glasses with military precision.

"Covert operations," nodded Grishin decisively. "You must have been unconscious when they rescued you. I knew this reconnaissance expert who was caught far behind the lines once. He was discovered and wounded in the head during a shootout..."

"No," interrupted Mironov, his tone grave. "And that's the truth. I remember dying, and the next thing I remember is arriving into Moscow with a small case of my belongings I left at the Bagram base."

Grishin shook his head emphatically.

"Look at him then," demanded Anna Nikolayevna, whose wits were coping much faster. "Just like winter of eighty-two. He doesn't look a day older."

"But that cannot be," said Grishin irritably. "There are no miracles in this life or the next. You know that, you silly old bitch. No, it was some secret crap..."

"It wasn't, Sergeant," replied Mironov steadily. "She is right. I am not a day older. And that's not all."

He stood up, unbuttoned his coat and pulled up the tunic beneath, pushing the trousers down slightly.

"I had appendicitis as a cadet," he said harshly. "They operated."

Grishin and his wife stared closely.

"There is no scar," she breathed.

"That's the way of it," answered Mironov. "That is all I know, but all of it is true."

Grishin peered at the spot closely.

"There is a very faded one, I think," he said without conviction. "Scars fade with time, you know."

They stared at each other, then Mironov restored his uniform and sat down.

"Do you... feel any different?" asked Anna Nikolayevna.

"Yes," said Mironov after a minute's consideration. "Yes. I am not hungry, I don't want to drink, I find it sickening to lie and I have no interest in women. I sat between the legs of a beautiful naked woman – and wasn't..."

"So is there anything you do feel?" asked Grishin, his voice trembling.

"An overwhelming compulsion to take revenge," answered Mironov. "I had come to Moscow because the bastards who sent us to our deaths are all here. I didn't know that, but it turns out be the case."

"I understand now," declared Anna Nikolayevna backing away. "You are a ghost."

"Perhaps," replied Mironov. "Perhaps. But you know, I feel more real than I did before my death. I can say one thing – I've never had such a sense of meaning. Maybe you are right – that does make me a ghost in Russia."

"Nonsense," exclaimed Grishin. "You were captured and nearly killed, then rescued and resuscitated in some secret facility. You suffered from loss of memory for a while and now you don't. That is the only possible explanation."

"Believe that if it helps you," replied Mironov. "But all that matters is that you agree with my purpose."

Grishin shook his head like a man clearing a hangover.

"No argument with that," he replied. "Just tell me

what we need to do. I am the chief of security at the Donskoi Bank, and there is no hardware that I can't get my hands on."

"Some bank," spat his wife. "More like a bunch of bandits."

"The best there is," confirmed her husband with a smile.

"How about the squad?" asked Mironov. "There should be a few of us left."

"Surely. I stay in touch with six out of the fifteen who survived, and the others will not be hard to trace. They will be mostly well and in excellent shape. Only the fit survive these days."

"Right," said Mironov. "We will organize everybody later. What I need from you right now is some hardware."

***

The day crew emerged from the building, scanning the street with guns drawn. Since Mashkin's warning was received and processed, life had become a tense experience for the security detail. They expected a large-scale assault any day.

A man once known as Captain Igor Nikolayev waited in the landing until waved into the street. He marched to the car without looking around, nodding to the guard who swung open the door. He delicately folded the tails of his camel hair coat as he sank into the back seat of a six-series Mercedes, bullet-proofed and reinforced against anti-tank missiles in a far-away German factory, no questions asked.

One street away a huge *KAMAZ* truck dumped its load of sand at a building site and rumbled into the street. The driver pulled the giant vehicle over to the curb and started to do his paperwork.

A short time later he looked up on mere instinct, seeing a machine pistol barrel levelled at him through the window.

"Go away," mouthed Mironov, nodding towards the other door. "Quickly and quietly."

The driver scrambled across the wide seat, plied open the opposite door and ran across the street, dodging oncoming traffic. Mironov climbed into the cabin and swept the hapless paperwork off the seat, placing his gun and a plastic bag beside him.

The truck ground a few gears and gathered speed. It rounded the corner just as a black Mercedes pulled out from the curb.

As the two vehicles were about to pass each, the truck swung across and smashed into the highly polished limousine. Not at all slowed down, its giant wheel rode over the shining black bonnet of the Mercedes, crushing it to a pancake.

The truck continued on, shattering the bullet-proof windscreen and squashing flat the driver's side of the saloon, rode down the Mercedes' trunk and bounced onto asphalt again. Mironov then smashed into the Jeep filled with guards, sending both occupants of the front seat through the windscreen.

His ear tuned to the screams from inside the Mercedes, Mironov flung open the door and hosed the remaining guards in the Jeep with a short burst of fire, killing them instantly. He jumped out of the truck and ran towards the Mercedes, gun in one hand and a plastic shopping bag in the other.

Quickly mounting the shattered bonnet, he emptied the clip into the thick windscreen, making a circle of bullet holes in cracked glass. He kicked the middle of the circle until it collapsed inside like a hatch.

A few shots came from somewhere in the intact side of the cabin, but they could only cause ineffectual cracks in the glass.

Mironov reached inside a plastic bag, removing a cluster of hand grenades tied by a single string through the pins. He pulled at the string, extracting the pins from all grenades at once The lethal projectiles tumbled back into the plastic bag.

His time running short, he pushed the entire bag through the circular hole in the windscreen and jumped off the shattered car, running to the truck as fast as he could. He was back in the cabin, driving away as the grenades detonated.

The truck was gathering speed when the blast wave caught its tail. The huge machine was flung across bitumen, fishtailed but kept going. A ball of flame washed harmlessly over its thick steel tailgate.

Mironov was moving in second gear, watching the burning remains drop on the road through the side mirror. His face was hard and taut as he left the scene of execution.

***

Berezov emerged from the doors of a fashionably exclusive restaurant, walking towards the car with some unsteadiness. He had a contented smile and was, apparently, pleased with his meal – a good state of mind for a man whose lifespan was now measured in seconds.

Concealed in a rooftop loft, Mironov gently squeezed the trigger, and the jacketed round burst from the barrel with a long tongue of orange flame. The silencer dampened most of the blast despite the extra powder which Mironov measured into the round. Only a dry crack was audible to those nearby – a pair of fat pigeons that burst in fright from the cornice.

The round traversed four hundred meters to its target and drilled the wrinkled forehead precisely in the middle, red cloud erupting from the back of the head. Then Mironov realized his predicament.

Instead of crowding around their fallen boss, the men standing next to Berezov instantly fanned out, weapons ready and totally oblivious to the fallen man. One of them accurately pointed in the direction from which the shot was fired.

Cursing at having taken such risks to merely deprive Berezov of one of his doubles, Mironov opened deadly fire on the running men. The first two went down without stopping, tumbling over the rough ground until the momentum of the sprint was dissipated. The rest instantly started to zig-zag, largely preventing further casualties.

By now Mironov was also running across the roof. He vaulted over the barrier into the stairwell and raced down the stairs.

He knew that coming from the roof as he was, he had no chance of beating them to the ground floor. He instead ran down a single fight of stairs and summoned the lift. Its rickety motor started overhead moments before feet began to pound on the concrete stairs to a rush of breathless voices below.

The lift arrived. His pursuers thundering up the stairs, Mironov jammed the doors of the lift with the blade of a combat knife from around his neck.

After that there was just enough time to splay himself at the top of the stairwell before the first of the attackers came into view, only to die mid-step. His comrades leapt back, down the stairs and out of Mironov's sight.

He knew their next move – to fire at him blindly, exposing only their wrists until ricochet off the marble ceiling found flesh. Mironov shook his head in annoyance, extracted a grenade from his pocket and pulled the pin.

The blind fire commenced as he expected, bullets

exploding over his head and pinging on the walls around him. Mironov waited for three seconds and dropped the grenade into the stairwell. He heard its metallic clatter on the stairs and flattened himself on the ground, covering both ears.

Even with palms tightly jammed against his skull he still found the explosion painfully loud. He waited with his finger hovering on the trigger, but there was no movement as dust settled.

Mironov crept back to the lift and pressed the button for the top floor. He retrieved the knife from the lift and jumped out as the doors creaked shut.

He made his way down as silently as the blood-streaked debris on the stairs allowed, past the shattered remains of what looked like six men. If there were any more, he hoped, they would scramble after the lift as fast as they can, taking little care in doing so.

No one charged him as he reached the ground floor of the building. But as soon as he stole outside, a flurry of masonry exploded around him as poorly-aimed bullets sprayed the wall. He dove to the ground and returned fire, killing two remaining protagonists who found themselves on the run without cover.

He was up and running again when a large Jeep crowded with men skidded into the courtyard.

Mironov discharged the rest of the magazine into its direction and dropped the rifle, now running for his life towards an unappetizing row of garbage containers. They stood next to a tall brick fence, a chance he had to take without knowing what lay on the other side. His planned escape route now cut off, that was the only direction left to him.

Mironov caused a sensation amongst the local community of cats, who scrambled from the garbage to escape his bulk leaping into their midst. He scrambled over the wall, automatic fire spitting on the brick around him, heaving his body over the brick wall. A few rounds whistled very close by as he cleared the wall and let go.

Mironov dropped to the ground heavily and grit his teeth at the pain of his knees slamming into the chest. He rose to a crouch and scanned the surroundings, scrambling to extract his pistol.

He was in a tramway yard, its ground criss-crossed with puckered metal tracks and littered with rusting parts. He ran to the nearest obstacle which could hide him entirely and fell flat. Finally concealed in relative security, Mironov gasped for breath and scanned the gloomy landscape, planning an escape route.

Mironov heard many powerful engines outside and realized that the yard was being circled by a large variety of pursuers. He made his way forward and climbed up the side of an old 1960's-styled tram, his feet sliding on the rusty ladder.

After looking around he decided to wait for darkness inside one of the trams. His pursuers clearly had no stomach for a search-and-destroy campaign. They probably hoped that he would make a run across open ground, to be cut down from a safe distance.

That strategy would not be entirely inoperable after dusk, but with every passing moment their conviction that he was still inside their cordon would diminish, as would the level of concentration required to take a moving target from long distance. Mironov climbed down to the ground, still breathing heavily as he recovered from his adrenaline-fuelled escape.

Before the light began to fade he was pleased to find an old cargo tram with a long, windowless hull. The old door was dented near the lock, and Mironov gently pushed it open, pistol in hand. Nothing was first visible in murky darkness.

Wrinkling his nose at the musty smell, he stepped inside and stood still, listening. He initially heard nothing, then became aware of faint and ragged breathing. He crouched, pointing the pistol at the source of that sound.

A tiny light flashed in the stuffy depth of the tram

– someone lit a wobbling candle. As Mironov's eyes became accustomed to the dark, he made out a child's face behind the flickering flame, eyes wide open in what he thought was fear.

As he stepped closer he saw a calm stare of desperation. He approached to see that the candle was held by a boy around ten years of age dressed in ragged clothing.

His face was painfully thin, further exaggerating the pain in the wide stare.

***

Many kilometres away a patch of virgin forest revelled in the majesty of winter dusk. Fir trees stood proud, clad in their majestic coats of glittering white. All was completely still but for occasional breaths of wind that caused snow to slide off low-hanging branches in absolute silence.

The sunset shadowed the snow with a pink undertone. There is nothing in creation to match the miracle of a winter forest.

Amid that forest stood a treeless hill, its abrupt tonsure justifying a nickname of Bold Mountain, by which it was known among Berezov's security detail. They were scattered in the forest at all times, concealed with consummate skill and undetectable to all but the most expert of eyes.

Berezov's mansion stood on top of the hill, a wrought iron fence around the elegant stone building being only a token of its defences. The stylish silhouette of its roof was broken up by numerous installations – tall antennae, satellite dishes, floodlights and a few sandbag emplacements, hastily added in recent days.

Berezov sat behind a gold-encrusted antique desk that once belonged to another oligarch of his long-suffering country, stirring sugar in a tall glass of tea inside a silver holder.

He was a tall, statuesque man with heavily

chiselled cheeks and a proud Roman nose. The eyes were faded grey, to match his very short hair. Grey theme was continued in a severe suit, grey with a hint of white stripe, and in faded complexion that was a tired veteran of many a sunburn.

The man sitting opposite him was younger, shorter and fatter. He was nearly bald, wisps of blond curls scattered untidily about the glistening scalp. He wore horn-rim glasses and a tattered sweater over what looked like an unwashed white shirt. His facial hues were the ruddy colour that comes of high blood pressure and the orange staining of nicotine. He was, however, completely at ease in the company of an elegant old warrior.

The latter could only shake his grey head.

"He came right through the defences," Berezov summed up the long tale he just heard. "I'd say our boys met their match."

"That's to be expected from time to time," replied his security head. Minin had cut his teeth in the KGB, rather than army, and he was comfortable with the idea of a campaign being a long chess game in which both sides lost pieces regardless of who won in the end.

But this equanimity did not please his boss, who swivelled towards him with expression of weary annoyance.

"Is that all you can say?" he asked irritably. "I wasn't the deceased's greatest admirer, but he was part of the organization from all the way back. We can't let a precedent like that become known. Every rat will be out to gnaw our toes."

"I can assure you on that point," said Minin comfortably. "We handled that part very well. I guarantee nobody knows about the Nikolayev affair except a handful of passers-by and the clean-up crew."

"Cops?"

"I had a friendly word with them. They just blocked the street whilst we loaded what remained of the cars onto tow trucks and drove off. Besides, I don't think any of them know who was killed. The official line is that Nikolayev is overseas on an extended business trip. As for the loss of the double – well, we nearly caught the assassin, and I am certain we will succeed next time. The first pancake is always a lump, as they say. No shame in that."

Berezov grumbled, nodding his head in reluctant acquiescence. Minin may not have acted fast enough to prevent this affair from blossoming, but he could certainly be trusted to put away all of its loose ends in his customary, systematic fashion.

"Any idea what this is about?" asked Berezov, his tone now more businesslike.

"In the absence of a better explanation," replied Minin slowly, his head nodding to the rhythm of his speech in contemplation. "I'd say this is exactly what we are told it is – a revenge for something that occurred in *Afgan*."

"But now?"

"Yes," acknowledged Minin. "A little difficult to account for, but not impossible. Things happen to people that can keep them away from their business."

"Nearly two decades?"

"Yes. We are not dealing with a normal individual. An elite soldier is no human being who merely put on a uniform for one reason or another – he is not really a part of our species any longer. A man of such will only ceases to be dangerous when he is reduced to a pile of ashes, and who knows – maybe when you train someone to be that wilful, even a physical death..."

"Oh, spare me," Berezov was one New Russian who did not rush into the mouldy embrace of Orthodox Church, a deeply troubled institution that still struggled to weed itself of KGB infestation. The onslaught of mysticism in the best-educated nation on earth was a source of ongoing amazement for the former general. His world remained an orderly structure of facts and figures.

Minin shrugged his shoulders. In his lifetime he has seen the absolute, scientifically demonstrable eternity of the Soviet regime evaporate like a dream induced by home-brewed liquor. If nothing else, Minin no longer believed in any such thing as absolute truth.

It wasn't as if he was particularly in need of God or heedful of His commandments – but as a matter of complete open-mindedness, Minin didn't care to rule God out, especially when there was no alternative explanation for the mess he witnessed.

"Why would such a resourceful individual wait so long for revenge?" asked Berezov glumly.

"Oh, numerous possibilities," replied Minin. "All quite mundane, really. Illness. Imprisonment, especially at the hands of foreign security services. Poverty. Amnesia after a head injury. Maybe he couldn't get back into the country before now. Maybe he was a respectable middle-class consumer somewhere in the West. Suddenly his beloved wife of the past fifteen years dies in a car accident along with their brood, so he launches himself on a suicide mission against us. Maybe he recovered some repressed memory from the war after visiting a psychiatrist for erectile problems. Maybe he was diagnosed with incurable cancer and decided to die in a more meaningful manner. I could speculate like this all day."

Berezov nodded in acknowledgement that such speculation did not merit further effort.

"So what do we know for a fact?" he asked impatiently.

Minin eagerly nodded and extracted a file from his briefcase.

"Mironov, Viktor Maratovich, born in Moscow, March 1950," he read in a jovial tone. "Father a hospital administrator, mother a nurse in the same hospital. Both killed in a bus accident whilst on holiday in the Caucasus, 1954."

"Little Viktor is uninjured, but left with only one living relative – mother's sister, who is still in a Gulag camp on statute 58-11 – conspiracy to commit a crime against the State. Sentenced in 1951 and released in 1958, but not rehabilitated or allowed to return to Moscow until 1969."

"On what basis?"

"Religious beliefs, apparently – she became an ardent Anabaptist in the prison camp. Even after Stalin's death, these people were still considered dangerous and handled rather brutally."

"Proceed."

"So after his parents' death Viktor is sent to an

orphanage near Moscow, and that seems to have been his first combat school. In November 1963 he stabs a supervisor in the stomach with a piece of window glass and, having thus disabled his victim, cuts off the man's penis. The motive, I suggest, is self-explanatory. His victim survives these considerable injuries but is dismissed from the post. There is no mention of Mironov being punished in any manner."

Berezov's eyebrows slowly rose in appreciation, and Minin read on.

"In January 1964 Viktor is sent all the way to the Suvorov Cadet School in Leningrad – by special order, document or contents not available on file. It is possible that he repeated the performance with broken glass with a less spectacular outcome, and his natural gift began to attract attention."

"As it must."

"Indeed. Or maybe they decided to ship him a safe distance away from the injured man's colleagues, perhaps to prevent them from settling scores."

"I suspect otherwise," Berezov's face creased in mirth. "Indeed, I would bet money they moved him to protect the remaining pederasts in the orphanage."

Minin acknowledged the point with a wry smile.

"Very possibly, General. Perhaps more in keeping with what we know now."

"Carry on."

"No incidents during the years in *Piter*. Mironov graduates with top marks in 1967. He is accepted into the Frunze Officer Academy, finding himself back in Moscow, where he meets his aunt for the first time since early childhood. Sporadic contact after that: a few letters, birthday calls and visits. He graduates in 1970, serves as a lieutenant in a rifle unit on the Amur border with China. Immediately distinguishes himself by stopping no less than seventeen infiltrators within a month. No survivors, predictably. Decorated in September 1971, details suppressed – I suppose the border problem never existed officially."

"Another of our unsung little wars," Berezov took a sip of tea. "What then?"

"In December 1971 Mironov is transferred to a *spetznaz* unit that is being trained for covert missions in Iran and Afghanistan."

"A difficult career move, being appointed to head a *spetznaz* unit right out of officer school."

"Not unheard of but certainly rare. No report of

any difficulties, however. Mironov's unit is kept busy with a number of low-key assassinations in Iran, then reconnaissance and a few acts of sabotage in Afghanistan. Rapid promotion to the rank of major by 1975, not bad for his age. He proves very effective in a campaign to sabotage what passed for infrastructure in Afghanistan, so USSR could offer to rebuild to our specifications."

"Even back then?"

"Oh, yes, general. From 1956 Soviet Union provided Afghanistan with various forms of aid, especially road construction. Almost no one noticed that the roads we built had the same steel-reinforced concrete as Soviet highways, being nothing more than a simple extension of our grid. The purpose of such sturdy construction was, of course, the ability to carry tanks. Why, we built these roads all the way to Khyber Pass and the Iranian border. Iran was to be attacked from two sides – from Afghanistan and from our own Azerbaijan. Within six weeks the Persian Gulf would have been in Soviet hands, but for the Iranian Revolution and a few other unfortunate coincidences, such as Reagan's election."

"That old dream I knew."

"As one may, being a senior commander in that operation. Back to Mironov: seemingly no personal life. Occasional visit to the aunt in Moscow, no wives, no children, no sport, no interests, no hobbies. No illnesses apart from a bout of appendicitis in the Suvorov, with an uneventful post-operative course. A number of broken bones, predictably, as well as the odd wound – also predictably. Non-smoker, modest drinker. Never joined the Communist Party, but not, apparently, because of political views. No one ever expressed concern about his reliability."

"An exemplary Soviet soldier," remarked Berezov acridly.

"More like a robot," replied Minin, shaking his head in wonder. "They wrote that most of his spare time was spent on weapons training and other such pursuits. A finely honed killer – hardly human. As I said, a different species."

Berezov rolled his eyes impatiently.

"At the start of the war in 1979 Mironov is already in Afghanistan as a military attaché, but takes frequent trips into the countryside on various errands. Plays a significant operational role in the coup d'état. During our subsequent fraternal assistance, otherwise known as the Soviet invasion of Afghanistan, he is placed in command of his original unit for... the rest of his life. He turns it into a roving special operation dedicated to interception of guerilla weapon convoys. Highly distinguished service again – commended for bold initiative and originality in command on numerous occasions, including by yourself, twice."

"I don't remember," said Berezov tartly. "By then my mind was already elsewhere."

"A pity. Mironov seeks and wins permission to use a squad of tanks instead of helicopters, arguing that to stem guerilla movements he must infiltrate the lesser-used passes and do so in an unpredictable manner. He commandeers a passing military artist, under whose supervision the squad repaints its tanks to blend in with local shingle. They complete the camouflage with old tents painted to the same pattern. The effect was to conceal his squad amongst rocks to any observer beyond three hundred metres. Mironov's strategy consisted of lying in wait in mountain valleys to intercept caravans carrying munitions. He would let the advance party go past, then blast the convoy with tank artillery. That proved more effective and less dangerous than helicopter patrols."

"A talented improvisation indeed."

"Evidently. I will skip various other endearments and decorations and come to the moment of his demise. His unit is ordered by you into a heavily defended mountain pass. Mironov objects, gets overruled, carries out the order. Loses most of his men but stays behind in a damaged tank and lays down covering fire to allow two machines to escape without further losses with seven surviving crew. Then apparently detonates the remaining ammunition in his tank, killing most of the guerillas involved in the ambush – I guess he had the last word after all."

Berezov nodded in contemplation. "Any more about that?"

"The site was inspected but no remains were found, as one would suppose – the tank magazine was still half-full. Posthumous Order of Lenin, funeral with full honours, then nothing, as one would reasonably expect. Until now."

"Continue."

"Furthermore, the survivors of his command include forty or so others, ranked private to captain, who were on leave at the time of Mironov's death or ended their service before. They are scattered all over Western Russia, and we have not investigated whether any of these are connected with his reappearance in any manner."

"That would take too many guns and too much time," commented Berezov. "It is more expedient to let them come to us, then interrogate the survivors. Let me see that paperwork."

Minin passed the file to Berezov, who opened it idly to look over a few photographs. The first was a faded shot of a plain-looking youth in a cadet uniform, but eyes staring at him from the yellowed print were two rifle barrels. Another photograph showed a grown Mironov in snow camouflage on skis, smiling somewhat artificially – the eyes still a double-barrelled weapon aimed at the camera.

Berezov carefully studied the last shot – a tightly sprung predator in dress uniform, receiving a decoration from a high-ranking officer Berezov vaguely recognized. Something to do with paratroops, but he couldn't quite remember and shook his head in annoyance.

"So is there a chance he'd cooperate with us?" mused Berezov. "I'd rather have a man like that on my payroll than kill him with great difficulty."

"Unlikely," replied Minin. "Unless you present a credible alternative explanation of the events that contributed to his... injury? Capture? Whatever happened to him afterwards."

Berezov thought about that for a few minutes.

"No," he replied with regret. "Such people don't listen to lies or make deals. They just kill. That weasel he roughed up said that Mironov knows about the heroin – no, I don't think he would negotiate with us now."

Minin raised his hands, palms upwards, in a

gesture of polite regret.

"Pity," he said thoughtfully. "It's never a pleasure to dispatch such talent."

Berezov looked up, his eyes light with bemusement.

"Mironov could end up dispatching us," he reminded impishly. "That would be an even greater pity, would it not?"

"I am certain that you jest, general," replied Minin politely. Berezov smiled back cryptically.

"A different species, you said," he commented, staring into his glass of tea.

Minin took his cues and bowed out. Berezov stared at the gilded carving on the door Minin closed behind him.

He still had a little time to kill until his mistress, a young beauty from Minsk with raven hair and sapphire-blue eyes finished her shopping. For some reason spending money made her even more over-sexed, something the former general could do with badly.

Like all Russian males of his generation, Berezov was not a good specimen of manhood, a once-hardened warrior in his early sixties looking far more geriatric than his soft-shelled Western contemporaries.

A lifetime of bad food, industrial-strength drink and smoking in total defiance of the consequences left him with only one organ that worked better as time went on – his brain.

That organ's function was framed by an ancient culture that ruthlessly left the lesser-educated and the lesser-witted to their devices in bitter cold, war and poverty. Berezov was an inheritor to a legacy that left him a complete master of his complex and brutal reality. As he moved through the jungle of his society he enjoyed an instinctive understanding of each and every nuance, which for lesser players was the only warning of sudden death, usually a second too late.

Now the master predator was puzzled. He was a typical product of the Russian underworld – an ironic name for a subclass which was now openly in charge of Russia. The latest criminals to rule that country did not bother with ideological or dynastic guises, much like Praetorian thugs who made and unmade Roman emperors centuries before.

Russia was not the only society suckled on Roman tradition, but the only one whose political culture still preserved it without dilution by subsequent invaders. The Mongols devastated and ruled Russia, but they were primitive nomads who wisely chose to remain at arm's length, using Russian clergy and aristocracy to do the dirty work.

When Turks toppled Byzantium, the last bastion of old Rome, Russia took the double-headed eagle of Eastern emperors as its emblem. Appropriately, it remained true to the ancient heritage of Roman skulduggery, despite Russian artists, scientists and engineers sitting astride the cutting edge of industrial civilization. A courtier from the time of Nero would feel completely at home in the Kremlin of today.

After the communist collapse the wheel of history turned a full circle to the twilight days of Roman glory - the body of a wounded empire lay exposed whilst criminals rampaged in the corridors of power.

The most frightening thought, mused Berezov, was that the criminal class appeared to be the only source of predictability. It seemed to be the sole reliable sector of the economy in a country whose flirtation with democracy left its vast expanse without any kind of government.

Most students of this phenomenon, himself very much included, looked back to Brezhnev's era as the golden years when control over citizens was absolute, starvation rare and the rest of the world trembled in fear of Soviet might, jumping at any opportunity to curry favour with USSR. Criminals had to conform to the framework of communist reality, open violence being largely the preserve of drunks and madmen.

The murder of his lieutenant shook Berezov hard, standing out as it did, even against the insanity of the present. There was no shortage of killers, but the boldness, the ruthlessness and the lateral thinking displayed by the attacker were exceptional.

It did not at all feel like the work of a freshly awakened amnesiac or a newly-released prisoner. With very rare exceptions such people were broken men who spent the rest of their miserable lives gulping fresh air.

No, this was the work of an elite operative who had lost none of his edge – much more likely a man who spent every day of the intervening years in a remote jungle, on the payroll of a tyrant engaged in some endless conflict.

There were plenty of such men who chose, after their Soviet reality collapsed, to follow the "banana trail" into tropical forests and deserts of former Soviet clients. They taught ungrateful natives of those environs that an empty rifle needs to be reloaded before it again becomes effective as a weapon, and, upon surrender to frustration, did the shooting themselves.

Berezov decided that whatever made the killer

wait so long for revenge was a distraction from the fact that he had to be stopped. Minin's foot soldiers would now scour Moscow until they came across that man's tracks, hunt him down and kill, preferably in a way that served as a warning to others.

A movement in the courtyard caught his eye, and he looked up in time to see his mistress arrive in a black Range Rover, followed by a similarly coloured Jeep crammed with armed men.

She swept out of the car into the dimming light, stunning in her stylish sable coat. The long black hair flowed down her shoulders as she walked her spring-loaded walk to the front door.

***

As his eyes adjusted to the musty darkness of the old tram Mironov saw that the boy holding the candle was emaciated to the point of being ethereal, the hand holding the candle almost transparent to the flickering light. He was dressed in ragged clothing a few sizes too large, his painfully thin arm sticking out of a torn sleeve of what might once have been a white shirt.

Mironov's gaze shifted when he heard soft wheezing coming from the floor, and he saw that the boy stood next to a makeshift bed of rags. An equally emaciated man lay on top of the filthy pile, his face contorted with suffering. Mironov came slightly closer and saw a trickle of blood escaping the thin mouth. Red-rimmed eyes stared past him without focus.

"We live here," said the boy tonelessly. "*Papa* and I."

"What's wrong with your father?" asked Mironov hoarsely.

The figure on the ragged bed shifted slightly, lifting the head and rising on one elbow.

"TB," he answered in a halting whisper. "Don't come any closer."

"Never mind," Mironov sat down next to him. "It's not a problem for me."

The man's eyes scanned him slowly, and the head of sweat-matted hair sank to the rags slowly.

"Big man," he said slowly. "New clothes, expensive pistol. I don't think you've come to the right place."

"It will do just fine," replied Mironov. "There are a few people outside I'd rather not meet just now. I'll wait until they lose patience, then leave you in peace."

"It doesn't matter," said the man. "Not for long, anyway."

"I see," Mironov told him grimly. "No chance?"

"No," the man laughed softly, breaking into a coughing fit. "I am on the way out."

Mironov nodded. "Let me sit with you."

"You don't fear being around death?"

It was Mironov's turn to chuckle.

"No, friend," he said grimly. "I've seen more of it than any man still living."

"War?"

"I've walked in hell."

The man nodded slowly.

"So many wars," he commented sadly. "Well, mine is nearly over."

"What war is that?"

"An ancient one – for survival. I was a teacher. Sat without a salary for five years. My family was starving, so I robbed a bank. They caught me a short time later: five years in a labour camp, three off for good behaviour."

Mironov nodded.

"Well, one year was all it took," the man continued. "I started coughing blood that winter. Everyone in my barrack had TB: you were either susceptible or you weren't. I was susceptible. Thank God, my Vanya isn't."

"Your son?"

"Yes. I am in a lot of pain and will be glad to die as soon as possible. My only regret is that I won't see what becomes of him. He will be a fine, fine man."

"No doubt," uttered Mironov through clenched teeth.

"None. Now, my wife – she took off and married

someone in Germany. Whore. Wanted to take Vanya with her, but he ran away at the last minute, and she had to leave without him. He returned two days later, with some food he managed to steal from a restaurant kitchen. The first proper meal I had in weeks."

Mironov nodded, listening intently.

"Stepan is my name," the man continued. "They put me on drugs in prison, held the disease for a while, but I couldn't afford a single day's treatment once they released me. That's why I was let out early, you know – the prison couldn't afford my medications either."

Mironov stole a glance at the boy, who sat by his father's feet, holding the candle and staring at the flickering flame.

"We lost our home," Stepan resumed, his voice now faint with fatigue. "Our old apartment block was bulldozed and replaced with quality American-style units for successful people. We slept on the streets, then found this place. Warmer than lying in the snow, but now it's only a matter of time, in any case."

Mironov nodded slowly, his expression part horror, part hatred.

"What did you teach?" he asked softly.

"History."

"Oh," Mironov nodded sardonically. "And what do you think of history now?"

"At first I thought it had stopped," Stepan answered slowly. "Then I realized I was wrong. It is actually going backwards. Russia is back in the Dark Age."

"You are wrong," retorted Mironov. "People had rules in the Dark Age. You see any rules now?"

"It's difficult," admitted Stepan. "But no, I think there are rules still. If people stop obeying them, it doesn't mean the rules disappear. It's just that a generation must pass before they are discovered again."

Mironov thought about this and shook his head in silence.

"So what's your story?" asked Stepan.

"I was a *spetznaz* officer," Mironov told him. "One of the best they ever spawned. My career consisted of killing, burning, torture and destruction until it was my turn. I was blown up in a tank, but next thing I knew I was in a train just outside of Moscow, two weeks ago."

"So you were badly wounded?"

"No, I was blown to dust. My tank was trapped and surrounded by the enemy, and I exploded it from inside."

"Where?"

"*Afgan*. Panshir valley – I even remember the coordinates."

"But we withdrew from there in Gorbachev's time! When did this... happen?"

"Fifteen years ago."

Stepan rose from the rag bed on both elbows and looked at Mironov intently for the first time.

"What happened in between?" he demanded, his voice now more resonant and possessed of a powerful timbre.

"Not a thing. I was simply dead, I had to be. Can you imagine a dozen tank shells detonating inside the tank? There is nothing left of the crew but vapour."

Stepan shook his head gently.

"That can't be right."

"Well, that's what happened," replied Mironov vehemently. "You can't survive an explosion that shreds your tank into shrapnel. But next thing I know I am on a train pulling into Moscow, wearing my dress uniform and with a suitcase of my meagre belongings from the base in Bagram."

Stepan stared at him, his eyes wide and white in the dim light.

"No mistake," reiterated Mironov. "I remember everything – no possibility of survival. Then the rest: my appendicitis scar has disappeared – I had it since I was a young man. Plus I feel totally different – I need only basic food, no alcohol and no women. My body feels about the same as when I was a cadet, and my mind is razor-sharp. I feel no fatigue and no fear. Something tells me I don't need to fear anything."

Stepan leaned back, staring at Mironov intently. A soft smile spread over his skeletal face.

"Superb," he said. "So there is something after all…"

"I don't know that," responded Mironov with an angry shake of his head.

"There has to be. Whatever it may be, you came from there. As if you were sent back."

"Maybe. Maybe it's just a void – and I simply failed to sink into it."

"A void… A nothing. A man returning from nothing. As they said in Latin, ex nihilo?"

"For all I know. And why not? What was I before I was killed – was that human life anyway?"

"So why are you here, or don't you know?"

"Oh, that I know. I am here to find the ones who did this to my men and kill them. There is no other thought in my head."

"More mayhem," said Stepan wearily. "Why couldn't they send you here to do something positive?"

"Because nothing can be positive as long as criminals are in charge," replied Mironov grimly.

Stepan thought about it for a while.

"That's what they all said," he replied with sadness. "All dictators, all usurpers, all inquisitors. We must destroy evil before we rebuild for good, they said. Well, they all destroyed. But the rebuilding always took centuries."

"It does," echoed Mironov. "It will."

"Very interesting," commented Stepan, falling back onto the rag bed. "How timely you are with this bit of information..."

They sat in silence for a while. Then Stepan rose up on his elbows.

"What is the practical use of that revenge now?"

"I don't know," replied Mironov. "But I know it is what I am now made of – there is nothing else left. I am going to hunt down the people who did this and kill them in some unpleasant manner. I am very good at this kind of work."

"And is that your idea of the highest purpose?"

"No," Mironov shrugged slightly. "But that is what I am here to do."

"I understand," replied Stepan after some silence. "Vanya!"

His son leaned closer.

"I want to speak to this man alone," Stepan told him. "Please leave us for a moment."

The boy stood up uncertainly, then walked to the end of the tram and trod down the stairs, shutting the rusted door behind him.

"Listen, Ex Nihilo," said Stepan, looking at Mironov with a new strength in his features. "I'd like to do some business with you."

"What do you have in mind?" asked Mironov, returning his stare.

"I want to rent that pistol of yours," Stepan reached into his ragged quilted jacket and proffered Mironov a small wad of dollars.

Mironov nodded, thought for a while and took the wad. He slid out the magazine, thumbed the top round to ensure that it was full and slapped it back. He checked the safety catch and handed the pistol, handle first, to Stepan, who eagerly grasped the shining metal and slid it under a makeshift pillow.

"One more favour," he said, his voice now strong and resonant. "Please ask my son to come in while you wait outside."

"Of course," replied Mironov, walking away without a glance.

He descended the rusty stairs, pushed open the door and cautiously stepped onto the ground. Vanya stood next to the tram and looked up at him expectantly.

"Your father wishes to see you now," Mironov told him gently.

The boy nodded eagerly and went inside.

Mironov stood still, feeling the rising wind as

daylight faded completely. A few despondent snowflakes drifted through the stilled air and landed on his burning forehead. The clouds parted, and the sinister light of the full moon lit up the yard, causing him to move into shadows.

Nearly an hour later he heard a squeal of the door, and Vanya returned to stand next to him, his gaze full of desperation and pain.

A shot rang out from inside the tram. Vanya began to cry, still staring ahead stiffly. Mironov put a heavy hand on his shoulder.

They stood like that for a while, then Mironov went inside and retrieved his pistol, wiping blood spatters from the barrel.

Vanya was still in the same pose when Mironov emerged. He looked up at Mironov and pointed at the tram questioningly, but Mironov shook his head.

"There is nothing for you there, Vanya," he countered sadly. "You father was a good man, but he is now gone."

Huge tears rolled down emaciated cheeks, but the boy hadn't moved a muscle.

"It's time to go," said Mironov. "Listen, I never had a father or a son. Think how lucky you both were. No matter what happens now, you know that your father was a good man who died to protect you."

"But he?..." asked Vanya uncertainly.

"Yes, he committed a crime," acknowledged Mironov. "But he did it for his family. Look around – men now commit crimes just to pass the time. It doesn't matter, Vanya. I would do everything your father did in the same circumstances."

The boy now wept openly, his thin shoulders shuddering inside the oversize shirt. Mironov dropped to his knees into snow, put both hands on bone-thin shoulders and stared into the boy's eyes.

By moon's putrescent light the cold, diamond-hard irises of a killer met an unfocussed stare of a grieving child – an instinctive attempt to transfuse their hardness to one whose childhood just ended, in the worst manner Mironov could imagine.

"You knew your father, Vanya," he said slowly and heavily. "He has died, but what your father was will live inside you forever. You are his son – carry that with pride. It is now your duty to honour his memory with courage."

When the boy's tears were exhausted Mironov let his hands drop to his sides. He remained on his knees, but his features flattened into an impassive mask.

"What did he tell you to do?" he asked in his officer's voice.

"He said to go to my aunt in St Petersburg, Tatyana Sergeevna."

"Do you know her well?"

"I think so. She stayed with us before *Papa* went to prison."

"Then you will do what your father told you, Vanya." Mironov stood up and took out Stepan's wad of dollars, pressing it into the boy's hand. "Get yourself to *Piter*. Are you able to do that?"

"Yes," replied Vanya firmly. "*Papa* was bed-bound for the past six months. I did everything for him."

"Good," said Mironov. "Now go."

"Goodbye," Vanya held out his tiny hand. Mironov shook it solemnly.

"He said to tell you," added Vanya over his shoulder as he walked away. "That what you are doing is probably wrong, but you will surely succeed."

Mironov did not reply and watched the boy leave. When Vanya was no no longer visible in the darkness Mironov removed the remaining grenade from his pocket, pulled the pin and tossed it inside the old tram, jumping backwards promptly.

There was a muffled roar of an explosion, and the cargo tram rocked on its rusted suspension. Flames started inside, and Mironov stood back, watching them rise.

Without a conscious reflection of what he was doing he stood at attention and snapped a salute to the flickering fire, then turned on his heels and ran through the yard.

Part II

It didn't take too long to find the men who accompanied Mironov to Yaroslavl. Their leader had, in fact, heard of Berezov's desire for information and approached Minin voluntarily. He knew the number from some past dealings.

Minin began the conversation with resigned patience appropriate to the magnitude of his task, but soon his face was burning with the obsession of a hunter who caught the first whiff of his quarry.

He learned that a man of neat appearance but no memorable features had joined a drug convoy, which later came under a withering attack in a forest ambush. The attack might well have succeeded, learned Minin, had the stranger not taken over command and with just a few terse orders turned the defectives defending the goods into an effective crew.

His description sounded very much like that of the rogue who assassinated one of the most protected men in Moscow with nothing more than a personal weapon and a handful of grenades – fewer weapons than carried by many a night watchman.

Then the trail ran cold. The suspect was introduced to drug runners by a Moscow whore. She contacted a local enforcer, who in turn directed her to the men running drugs to Yaroslavl. The whore was not unknown in that district, but she hasn't been seen for some days since – dead, more likely than not.

Further information about her was sought, but it turned out that she did not use a regular address for work. Just on the safe side, Minin put out a word that he wanted to talk to her.

Once again his network performed faultlessly, and Nina learned of his interest the same night. She played the message on her machine time and time again, with increasing horror. She finally put down the handset and sat down on the floor, crying soundlessly into her hands.

Which was how Mironov found her when he returned from a rendezvous with Grishin.

He tapped her on the shoulder, but she didn't react. He persisted, and she dropped her hands, looking up with red-rimmed eyes.

"I don't blame you," she said tonelessly, her voice hoarse and broken. "It's just that I don't know what to do next."

He took her hands and pulled her up, increasing his force until she complied, walked her to the sofa and made her drink an ounce of vodka.

"Explain," he ordered evenly.

"They traced me back to the call about

Yaroslavl," she said. "About your little jaunt in the country."

He nodded in comprehension and looked to her to continue.

"There's nothing else to do," she concluded miserably. "I am a dead woman."

"You can just leave," he said in the same even tone. "I can give you money."

"No," she whispered, and the tears started again. "I can't leave Moscow."

They stared at each other for a while.

"I am going to talk to them," she said slowly.

"They will probably kill you," replied Mironov.

"If I can't stay, I might as well be dead," she told him, rising with determination. "I have to do it. End of discussion."

"Very well," said Mironov. "What can I do to help?"

"Leave," she replied unhesitatingly. She stood up, pulling her nightgown over her head. Turning away from Mironov, she walked into the bathroom and shut the door. He heard the shower come on and stood up, thinking. Then he marched to the bathroom and rapped on the door loudly.

"What?" she shouted irritably.

He opened the door a fraction, hearing the shower stop.

"Just one thing," he said evenly. "Don't contact them until tomorrow. Understand?"

"All right," she replied tonelessly. "It won't make any difference."

The water started again.

Ten minutes later he stood in the shadows of a nearby park, his suitcase at his feet. He was reasonably certain that all traces of his presence were removed from the apartment except fingerprints, if it should come to that – but he had no intention of offering his fingers for comparison.

He pulled out his phone and called Grishin.

"It's time," he said harshly. "Get everyone together."

Grishin started to voice his thoughts, but Mironov's phone began to beep at regular intervals to indicate a flat battery. Grishin said that he understood and rang off.

Mironov shook his head in annoyance, pocketed the phone and sat on the bench out of the light. He waited, invisible to any casual observer.

Not an hour later the park came alive with men who moved like shadows as they gathered under the bare bows of a huge oak tree. Grishin took out a silenced pistol and fired, with barely a glance, at the nearby light and immersed the group into a cloud-dampened moonlight.

Taking this as his cue, Mironov emerged from the shadows. He put down his suitcase and removed a small field torch from his pocket, pointing it towards him. There was a collective gasp as he thumbed the switch, illuminating his face.

As one man, they jostled into a rough line, stood at attention and saluted. Mironov snapped his heels together, thrust his hands to the sides and stood still for a few seconds. His right arm then rose to the visor of his officer's cap, hovered there for a while, then shot down.

The line remained at rigid attention.

"At ease," said Mironov hoarsely.

***

Hidden in a rusty van painted with a florist's emblem, they watched as a Mercedes and two Jeeps parked inside Nina's courtyard. Men clad in black leather jackets spilled from the cars, and four marched inside the building. Mironov brought a hand-held radio towards his mouth.

"They are here," he said tersely.

"I see them," came the reply.

Then there was a long silence. One of the men left by the cars lit a cigarette, blowing smoke into the wind.

"What's happening?" asked Mironov after a while.

"Not a lot," came the reply. "A few raised voices, but nothing to worry about so far."

One of Mironov's men had a parabolic microphone at the door of the flat. His partners stood one landing above, ready to loose with machine pistols in case the conversation inside turned ugly.

Some twenty minutes later the radio came alive.

"It's not good," said the man with the parabolic microphone, moving up the stairs away from the door. "They are taking her away for what that scum called a proper interrogation."

"Right," replied Mironov. "Follow them down but stay inside. Cut off their escape."

He glanced at the men left on the street and picked up the radio again.

"Volodya," he said into the unit. "Take them out."

The shots themselves were inaudible, but both guards lolling outside the Jeep collapsed, sliding to the ground along the side of the vehicle. The third tore open his jacket to reach for a weapon, but his head exploded in a cloud of red spray, body whirling into a snowdrift.

Four men in black overalls ran to surround the exit, weapons drawn.

Nina came out of the unit clad in a torn dress, a coat thrown over her shoulders. There was a fresh bruise under her left eye.

The men flanking her on both sides lived for another second, taking direct hits from silenced pistols to the sides of their heads. The last nearly made it back into the door but was thrown backwards by a shot from inside, collapsing on top of his fallen comrades.

Nina stood very still until Mironov slid open the door of the van and walked towards her.

"Go get a few things," he ordered.

She nodded and disappeared inside. One of Mironov's men stripped the corpses of all valuables. He stood up showing the keys to Mironov.

"Leave the tub," said Mironov, referring to the Mercedes. "Let's go."

Nina emerged from the front door dressed in boots and jeans under a drab ski parka. She hefted a small backpack, which one of Mironov's men took from her with deference.

The convoy of rag-tag vehicles left only a quarter of an hour after the first shots were fired, leaving corpses to ooze blood into snow. The police cautiously waited another hour before arriving to begin the clean-up.

Nina stared forward in the seat beside Mironov, her face totally expressionless.

"Maybe it's fate," she said all of a sudden.

"I don't think I follow," replied Mironov politely.

"It doesn't matter," she waved her hand dismissively. "Not any more."

"Very well," he said gently. "You can tell me as much or as little as you wish."

"Maybe afterwards," she replied, her tone slightly warmer. She took his hand and held onto it with both of hers. He relaxed his fingers and soaked the strange sensation of warmth coming from her skin. Mironov squeezed a little, and she reciprocated.

Nina leaned her head against his shoulder and sighed under her breath. A moment later she fell asleep, oblivious to the rest of their journey through the outskirts of Moscow.

***

There was plenty of room for men inside the old *dacha*, a country retreat of a forgotten Stalin-era official, who built this sprawling house in a birch forest fifty kilometres away from the city. They had more trouble hiding their cars, only three of which fitted inside the cavernous shed.

Axes and shovels were used to cut a car-sized hole in the snow to frozen ground, and the trophy Jeeps were parked with only the roofs visible above the snow. A tarpaulin was hastily thrown over them and covered with loose debris.

The old commandos made themselves comfortable in the vast house. Grishin said that the current owner had left the country after a dispute with the tax police had turned nasty, leaving a few corpses from a bungled raid. There was no concern that anyone would rush to investigate ongoings on his former property.

Two men drove out to the nearest town to buy food and drink.

Mironov led Nina down the corridor in the bedroom wing, sensing that the most distant door led to the master bedroom, where Stalin's henchman once bedded compliant women.

To his relief the decorations were plain and rustic, matching the walls of pine logs. A large bed stood facing a wide window, and in the corner he saw a fireplace, complete with a basket of firewood and a pile of old newspapers. Everything was covered in thick dust from the chimney.

Mironov knelt on the floor and quickly laid a fire. He used his combat knife to make kindling, rather than burn newspapers, lit the fire from a single match and gently blew on the nascent flames until they began to devour dry wood. He then straightened and turned to Nina.

She sat still on the bed, staring into space. Mironov walked towards her slowly, gently took her hands and led her to fire, sitting her down on his coat thrown over the floor. She slowly stretched her arms towards the fire but her gaze remained vacant.

"I must leave now," he said quietly. "Get some sleep."

"Come back," she replied hoarsely. "Wait with me until they come."

"Who?"

"You know very well who."

"No," said Mironov. "They won't be coming. Their rampage is over. This is now a war, and wars I win."

"People die in wars."

"Oh yes," replied Mironov, rising from the floor. "But not twice."

He allowed his hand to linger on her shoulder and left her in front of the flickering fire.

Gently closing the door behind him, Mironov marched down the corridor to the main room of the *dacha* – a wide glassed-in alcove looking out onto the forest. It was brightly lit with a number of ceiling lights, and a huge fire was roaring in the corner. On a low coffee table he saw a case of vodka, a brand he had never heard of. Plastic glasses were being passed around as he entered.

All chatter immediately ceased, and every man stood up. Mironov took a plastic glass, and with the other hand hefted a bottle out of the case, twisting off its top with a practised movement of thumb and forefinger of the same hand. He dropped the cap on the floor and crushed it with his heel.

When all glasses were full the men stood in respectful silence, looking at him with anticipation. Mironov swallowed hard and raised his glass.

Snapping to attention, he downed the vodka. It was an old military tradition – amongst servicemen the memory of fallen comrades was toasted with silence.

The men followed suit, and the glasses were

immediately refilled.

"To comrades who returned," said Mironov simply and tossed the contents of the glass down the throat again.

There was a rumble of approval, and every man in the room copied his movement in unison. Grishin emerged from the ranks and looked at Mironov questioningly. Mironov nodded his permission.

"To the comrade we didn't expect to meet on this miserable earth!" shouted Grishin hoarsely, raising the glass towards Mironov before throwing it down. He then crossed himself and bowed to the east, in gratitude to the God he found in his old age.

"Thank you, Sergeant," replied Mironov. "Now let's proceed to business. Comrades, there were many injustices in life and even more for us, veterans of an unpopular and a forgotten war. But one such injustice we have an opportunity to redress."

***

The next day Mironov and Grishin took a few men in the stolen Jeep. They skirted Moscow, carving a path to a drab town standing in the shadow of an industrial estate, a sprawling plant surrounded by grime and barbed wire.

They drove down the main street of the town, a wide avenue of cracked concrete that was once designed to take the weight of heavy trucks. It was flanked by box-like three-story houses, constructed from similar material and little better maintained. Apart from the occasional curtain, flower box or faded washing, the buildings completely lacked individuality.

"Look," Grishin pointed to the roof of the nearby apartment block.

"What is it?" asked Mironov.

"The chimney," replied Grishin.

Mironov immediately understood. There was nothing, not even a wisp of smoke, emerging from the rooftop exhaust of the building's boiler. He looked across to the next house and the one next to that.

"They are dead out of business," said Grishin grimly.

Mironov nodded, having understood what the

asking price of his desire could be. The entire town couldn't pay for its heating oil. Its citizens – those who had nowhere else to go – were now in their beds, preserving what body heat they still had. It was a slow way to die.

The Jeep rolled to the factory fence, and Mironov got out in front of the locked gate. At his signal the driver sounded the horn, its foreign sound drifting across the dirty expanse of the factory, cluttered with what looked like abandoned machinery.

An elderly man emerged from the guardhouse, hastily donning heavy gloves. He walked across the frozen ground gingerly, a habit borne of many slips and falls in a place where a broken hip left one with no alternative but suicide or an ugly death.

He stopped on the other side of the gate, his wrinkled face covered with stubble. He was no more than fifty, but grey eyes surrounded by rheumy lids showed fatigue that was older than time.

"Who is in charge here?" asked Mironov briskly.

The guard suddenly cackled, the remains of yellow teeth bared in mirth.

"You are," he replied, unerringly pointing to where Mironov wore a concealed weapon.

Mironov shook his head sourly.

"Who owns this place?" he asked without a change in tone.

"You do," replied the guard even more pointedly, his wide-swept hand gesture indicating that he was only partly joking.

Mironov processed this information in silence.

"Is the plant in running order?" he asked curtly.

"It was, until the generators ran out of fuel," replied the guard with bitterness, no longer troubling to conceal his true feelings. "We had to use something to heat our houses."

"Fine," said Mironov. "Where is the foreman?"

Five minutes later he and Grishin strode through the gates. The guard was taken back to town in a Jeep to seek out the foreman. Grishin was engaged in an animated telephone discussion with a supplier of crude diesel of the kind used by the factory generator.

The Jeep returned bearing the foreman – a better-kept version of the guard who stared at Mironov with obvious desperation.

It soon transpired that the local electricity

substation had expired at the start of winter frosts and was unlikely to ever be rebuilt, given that the plant was presently tooled to produce a very outdated model of its product. That model was tailored to the custom of some hapless third world client, whom Soviet sponsors chose to deprive of something more modern in line with some long-forgotten global intrigue.

Unfortunately for locals the Soviet Union ceased to exist shortly afterwards, leaving the plant tooled to manufacture an obsolete product and no money whatsoever to upgrade. Demand slid to naught shortly afterwards, and deaths started as soon as the first snow fell.

"I want you to get your men together," said Mironov. "There is a tanker of fuel and a truckload of food on the way. Can you do a small production run with what you have?"

The foreman thought for a while, his fingers assisting him with mental calculations.

"Yes," he said at last. "I can do everything except spray the paint."

"Unnecessary," replied Mironov.

"In that case I think we can manage," said the foreman. "We will start in the morning. None of my people saw a square meal in weeks. "

"No hurry," replied Mironov. "Tomorrow will be fine."

Later that day the oil tanker left most of its load in the factory's fuel tank and topped up the buildings with the rest. Mironov's men set up a canteen in the assembly hall of the factory, still bedecked in crimson banners bearing the catch-cries of the Soviet era.

Warm for the first time since autumn, the workers and their families – all elderly people without the means of moving to more viable communities – ate their first proper meal in a longer time than any cared to recall. There was a liberal supply of food and a measured quantity of vodka, not to mention the first glimmer of hope of surviving to spring.

The foreman broke up the merriment just after ten o'clock, and Mironov's men camped inside the hall apart from a sentry, who spent an uncomfortable night inside the guardhouse – just in case.

The next day the generator fired up without a hitch, machines began to turn and trolleys laden with feedstock rolled from frozen stores. The production run took exactly sixteen hours, then the product was loaded into hastily assembled wooden crates.

At midnight a large truck with a logo of a furniture removalist pulled up at the factory gates. Grishin embraced a man who jumped from the cab, then the vehicle rolled inside and was carefully loaded by hand.

They followed the truck back to the Stalinist *dacha*, where it was unloaded hastily. The driver was evidently pleased to see the end of the transaction and disappeared, clutching his pay.

The man who embraced Grishin stayed behind. Indeed, there was now a decided lack of sleeping space inside, with Mironov's men being joined by comrades from other units. Grishin did not refuse anyone he knew, so long as each man had current experience with weapons and reason to be angry at the way the empire treated veterans of an inconvenient war.

Mironov was going to use the remainder of his money to hire some technical experts, but this proved redundant. In fact, his numbers were such that security and maintaining a proper chain of command were now more urgent considerations.

When the blizzards of December heralded the imminent approach of the festive season, Mironov found some skis in a shed and took the factory product into the snow-bound forest for a test.

When he was about three kilometres away, he

followed the terrain into a ravine. A frozen river zigzagged at the bottom, and he traced the river's course until he came across a massive trunk of a fallen pine whose remains were embedded in the ice. Its roots protruded from the frozen surface, regally coated in snow.

Stopping four hundred paces away, Mironov unravelled a light shoulder-fired anti-tank missile, an older model whose linear charge was somewhat suspect in design. At one time Mironov's unit was almost sent to Iran to prepare the ground for the Soviet invasion, mainly by shredding Iranian war planes as the opening salvo of the campaign. Mironov found the missile a powerful, easily portable weapon, and he was briefly deployed to the factory to help rectify its known faults.

He now extended the rear of the weapon to form a shoulder stand, cocked the bright copper tube and brought it to his shoulder. He aimed through the upright sights, weapon resting with comfortable familiarity in his grip, then gently squeezed the brushed metal of the trigger.

A blinding orange streak hurtled through a white landscape and slammed into the fallen tree. For a split second nothing happened – the fuse allowed half a second for the impact to deliver full penetration.

Then there was a giant thump, and the fallen

trunk disappeared in a burst of bright yellow and red. Even at that distance Mironov was nearly thrown off his feet by the blast, and a split second later thunder rent the air, loud enough to make Mironov's ears ring painfully.

He dropped the smoking shell, hearing it hiss in the snow, and he looked around.

The winter landscape was cleft by a wound, mud and water sprayed over snow from a large hole in the ice. The pine was nothing more than a scatter of splinters, the last of which were still fluttering to the ground around Mironov.

He nodded thoughtfully and turned around on his skis, working his jaw to release the painful spasm in his ears. A smile through clenched teeth creased the lower half of his face, but his eyes remained dead, glittering lenses of a machine that rolled towards its lethal purpose.

***

At Nina's request, she was twice given a considerable sum of money and driven to the edge of Moscow, where she disappeared inside the metro. On both occasions she refused an armed escort to her destination, returning some hours later and in a considerable state of distress.

She refused to say anything and smiled with sadness when Mironov suggested that there was no problem in her life which he could not solve now that he was in charge of a lethal private army.

She shook her head sadly and turned away to stare at the fire.

"You believe that every problem can be solved by sufficient force?" she asked at length.

"If the force is indeed sufficient," replied Mironov without hesitation.

"Time will tell if you are right," she replied.

Later that night the country shuddered to a halt. In the Russia liberated from the communist yoke there are three major celebrations clustered at the end of December. Initially there was only New Year, which under Bolsheviks replaced traditional Christmas, keeping all of its trappings bar the religious aspect.

Then Christmas returned, being celebrated in the

first week of January, as Russian Orthodox Church still runs on the Gregorian calendar, two weeks behind the rest of the world. Finally, as part of Russia's globalization, Western Christmas was added to the start of that procession, more as an excuse to celebrate, rather than as an expression of ecumenicism.

That year's festive season heralded the approach of the seventh year since the armoured façade of the Soviet Union dissolved into toxic rubble. It was entirely clear to any sober observer that democracy was making things worse rather than better, and for that reason most observers hastened to end their sobriety.

Moscow went quiet, its insane traffic ebbing as people hurried back to their cramped homes. White tablecloths awaited their return, laden with a traditional feast – vodka with cucumbers and marinated mushrooms, salads prepared from canned ingredients and, as of recent times, relatively fresh meat in relative abundance.

One undeniably positive outcome of the Soviet collapse was an immediate restoration of Russia's food supply in all its traditional glory. Those able to swim with the tide of their new society at least had the means of laying on a traditional feast, even if the process was not as simple as walking into a Western-style supermarket.

As shadows lengthened what little traffic was left on the streets that Christmas Eve consisted of expensive foreign vehicles, ferrying those who gorged themselves on the carrion of Soviet power to lavish parties hosted by equally glamorous figures.

Mostly, these cars were black. An old tradition which survived the collapse of communism endowed a black car with significance of a high rank in government or, more ominously, an affiliation with the security apparatus. Now exclusively of foreign manufacture, large black vehicles hurtled through dimly lit streets barely cleared of snow, their passage marked by fountains of dirty slush that was dodged by pedestrians with muffled curses.

Mironov sat in the back of a very different car, an older *GAZ* borrowed from one of Grishin's friends. All of these sturdy vehicles are painted khaki, and it took considerable eye for detail to note that the number plates, sprayed with hair lacquer and liberally sprinkled with sand, were civilian rather than military.

Mironov was stunningly attired in his dress uniform, which he hadn't worn since the day of his arrival to Moscow.

Even in that sorry age when scavengers clad in pinstripe were admired as role models by young Russians, his uniform had a mesmeric effect in a nation that had spent an entire millennium at war. There will never come a time when a crowd of Russians would fail to cease its banter, listen and instantly obey any order a crisply-uniformed officer of their imperial army barks in their direction.

Mironov counted on that now.

Grishin pulled up outside one of the few old-fashioned mansions left in Moscow from the nineteenth century. Sandwiched between vile buildings of the Soviet era, it was discretely separated from the street by a tall wrought-iron fence skilfully blended with the sprawling garden. It belonged to an African mining company whose directors worked hard to protect the flow of rare minerals to the Russian space industry, and the building enjoyed sufficient protection even after the Soviet rule collapsed. Some things in Russia changed only in name.

A red carpet flowed over a staircase leading to the circular drive. Grishin stopped opposite the red strip, nodding to Mironov in reassurance. A truckload of his men was stationed around the corner.

Mironov slid out of the back seat imperiously, nodding curtly to the magnificent African maitre'd who opened the creaking door with a polite bow. Straightening his uniform with a sculptured gesture, Mironov marched up the marble steps towards a bevy of armed guards, soft sounds of a Beethoven quartet beckoning from the warmth inside.

"I have an urgent message for Mr Arumov, who is believed to be a guest," he said to the thug dressed in a uniform resembling that of American police. The thug stepped to block Mironov's path and put one hand on the holster of his gun importantly.

"Papers," he demanded in an insolent tone.

Mironov stared at him for a few withering seconds, then put his right hand into the breast pocket of his tunic covered with medal ribbons. He extracted a military passport and splayed it open on the photograph page.

The thug reached for the passport, but Mironov yanked it away.

"The interior pages of this document are classified, retard," he barked loudly. "If you get to see what's inside, you will have to be taken into military detention until my current project is finished, except I don't think you would survive that long behind bars."

"Then you can fucking well turn around and leave," announced the thug proudly.

Mironov leaned forward, his eyes pure menace.

The thug shrank back instinctively.

"Listen, village idiot," hissed Mironov, snatching a mobile telephone from his trouser pocket. "If I press this button and call that number, you will be arrested for interfering with state investigations. Do you even know who I am?"

The thug shook his head with increasing uncertainty.

"I don't want any Western booze or any dirty women or whatever the fuck else you have in there," continued Mironov, smoothly changing the subject. "I am here on government business, to speak to a man who has the bad taste to be one of the guests. I will speak to him very soon, or you will find yourself under arrest, and I promise you will not enjoy what follows. Got that?"

He thumbed a button which flashed a number prearranged with Grishin. The backup plan was to storm the party directly, but that was bound to be a very messy manoeuvre, and it was prayed that bluff would work in the first place.

It did. The thug attempted to save face by offering to find the relevant man and to invite him outside, but Mironov gave such a vague description that the idea died a quick death, and Mironov was waved inside with resignation.

"Wise move, child," barked Mironov as he was being patted down at the door. "You have no idea how much trouble you just saved yourself."

The thug nodded compliantly.

"Next time you see this uniform," continued Mironov as other security guards stepped out of his way. "Cross the street and run like hell."

Curtailing a perfunctory body search, the second thug stepped away from Mironov gingerly.

"There are still patriots in our armed forces, and we will not allow this brothel to run for much longer," announced Mironov venomously, pointing at the emblem on the thug's breast pocket. "God help you if we find you in this clown suit when we return to the streets."

The guards stared at the emblems of their security company instinctively, knowing that Mironov referred to its owner, a minister in the current government.

"When you see us coming take it off and hide naked in the snow. Frostbite will be nothing compared with what my men will do to despoilers of Motherland."

He replaced the phone in his pocket and marched inside, removing his peaked cap and carrying it over his left arm, as required by protocol. His back was held rigidly straight until he was well inside the whirl of exquisitely dressed bodies. There his manner gradually transformed until he was looking a little sheepish and inconspicuous in the crowd, just a middle-ranking military lackey out of his depth, moving through the crowd of super-rich with a naïve smile.

He accepted a glass of champagne and spilled half of into a pot plant whilst pretending to squeeze past a circle of men surrounding an ambassador of an African country who was resplendent in his multicoloured robes. Mironov continued to navigate through the party, managing to pretend he was on the way elsewhere whenever anyone attempted to converse with him, until he spotted the target.

Arumov was a squat man of Azeri extraction, whose olive skin and coal-black eyes instantly reminded Mironov of Afghanistan, and he clenched his teeth in anger.

Arumov was dressed in a dark suit which matched his complexion immaculately. He was rocking on his Gucci-clad heels, engaged in frivolous conversation with a number of stunning-looking women half his age.

Mironov moved away and struck up a few conversations with older women, evidently deserted by their philandering husbands in pursuit of younger flesh. He vaguely answered questions about service in the Guards' tanks, airily mentioning a desert terrain, foreign consultancies and other romantic notions until he saw Arumov bow to his companions and move towards the clearly labelled toilets.

Mironov made his excuses and slid through the crowd in pursuit, entering the toilet just as Arumov leaned over the basin to wash his hands.

When he straightened Mironov sprang to cover the remaining distance between then, whipped his hand in a choke hold around Arumov's throat and held rigid index and middle fingers in front of the man's eyes, ready to stab them out. Arumov tensed his arms, but Mironov's hand tightened hard on his throat, and he went limp in acquiescence.

"Listen very carefully," said Mironov quietly, calmly and slowly, something he long ago learned terrifies and disorientates frightened men more than loud threats. "I am about to place an object in your pocket."

He extracted his mobile telephone and slid it into the inside pocket of Arumov's jacket. The panic in the man's eyes receded.

Mironov then produced another device, which looked like a crude remote control with a single button encased in a plastic cover. Mironov flipped open the transparent case and held it aloft, fingers well away from the red button, to ensure that Arumov saw it in the mirror.

"The phone I just placed in your pocket contains one hundred grams of Semtex," he explained to Arumov, seeing the man's dark eyes widen in horror. "It should be more than enough to make your top half unrecognisable. Understand?"

Arumov nodded furiously.

"This is the detonator. Come with me if you don't want to die in that very spectacular manner, keep your hands away from your breast pocket and do precisely what I tell you."

Arumov nodded, and Mironov's arm slowly relaxed its grip, then dropped away, as if releasing a precious object just balanced in the correct position.

They walked out of the toilet, Mironov opening the door for his companion deferentially.

"Unfortunately, the matter I just described requires your immediate attention," he announced loudly, speaking with a rude Southern accent. "My chauffeur should be waiting outside."

Arumov nodded mechanically and walked to the wardrobe, being handed his coat. Mironov grasped the collar of the coat and held it out, as if assisting a more important man. Arumov slid into the coat awkwardly.

Thankfully, Grishin really was waiting outside, now dressed in camouflage uniform and at the wheel of the *GAZ,* now with a blue beacon slowly rotating on the roof. He turned the beacon to full speed as Mironov opened the door for Arumov and waited for the man to climb into the back seat.

Then Mironov jumped into the front. The *GAZ* rolled out of the circular drive, accelerated and disappeared into the festive night.

Arumov watched with dismay as they sped past his limousine, the chauffeur smoking at the kerb with his back to the street. Arumov's body guards were nowhere to be seen – not being allowed into his party, they probably left to improvise another. They would not expect their master to tire of womanising and drinking until a much later hour.

Arumov's extensive experience was not required to deduce that all of this was known to his captors in advance.

They drove through a few industrial suburbs, Arumov maintaining silence, which indicated that his self-control had returned. A while later Mironov turned around in his seat, detonator in the left hand as he held out the right. Arumov removed the telephone from his pocket and placed it in

Mironov's hand.

Mironov calmly nodded to Grishin, who sped up.
Mironov rolled down the window and tossed out the
telephone, then waited a few seconds and pressed
the red button of the detonator.

Arumov involuntarily turned around to see a
bright burst of flame at the side of the road. They
were travelling too quickly to feel the blast, but the
sound caught up with them a second later – a
menacing, low-pitched thunderclap that rattled the
ill-fitting windows.

Arumov's composure was gone in an instant.

"What the fuck is this?" he shrieked at Mironov.
"You have any idea who I am, *mudaki*?"

"But we do," hissed Mironov, his face suddenly
contorting with hatred. "Djarjat Ibrahimovich
Arumov, lieutenant, helicopter wing, Guards. A
disgrace to the uniform if ever there was one.
Berezov bailed you when they caught you playing
with little boys in *Afgan*, didn't he?"

Arumov listened to this recitation in mounting
terror.

"And that was the beginning," continued
Mironov hatefully. "Some paperwork got lost in
exchange for many favours. A few transport flights,

then what? More boys for being a go-between with *Duhi*?"

One glance at his victim was sufficient to confirm the truth of that allegation.

"Then wealth," continued Mironov. "Dollars for you, remains of your comrades-in-arms for vultures, correct? Then more boys whilst you peddle Berezov's drugs in Russia?"

The anger in Arumov's dark eyes suddenly faded, and he sat frozen still, too frightened to react.

"Ah," said Mironov, addressing Grishin. "I think this vermin just figured out who I am. Didn't you, vermin?"

He swivelled a pistol to point between Arumov's eyes, which widened even further.

Grishin pulled into a deserted factory through wide-open gates. A few hours earlier his men had swept it free of various wildlife, and Grishin's posture relaxed as he parked in front of a soot-stained building with broken windows.

They frogmarched Arumov inside, where his wrists were cuffed above his head. Mironov quickly threaded the link of the cuffs over a hook hanging from the ceiling, and someone worked the crank in the darkness, lifting Arumov off the ground. Grishin lit a railroad lantern, which he placed on the ground.

Mironov began to undress in front of the lantern, moving slowly and deliberately. He reverentially stowed his dress uniform in an old suitcase he brought from Bagram. From the same case he removed a camouflage uniform, similar to what he wore on his last day in Afghanistan.

The cloth was better, he noted in passing, but the desert pattern hasn't changed, probably in anticipation of the next war in the same region. Wheels of history moved round and round.

He finished dressing and buckled a heavy belt around his waist, clipped on a holster and stood before Arumov just as he might have stood before him a decade and a half ago, in the middle of a rocky Afghan plane.

"Here I am," he said grimly. "Just like the old days, right?"

Neither seeking nor awaiting any response from the prisoner, he whipped out the combat knife from a sheath, worn around the neck as his personal signature. The blade slashed at Arumov with inhuman speed.

There was a scream as the expensive silk shirt split open, a little blood staining its textured pattern. A mass of pink, worm-like intestines dropped from the stomach heavily, and Arumov fainted, sagging on the outstretched arms.

Mironov splashed him with icy water from a dirty bucket on the floor and waited patiently. Arumov opened his eyes a few minutes later and issued a long, bubbling scream of abject terror. Mironov waited for the sound to die, staring at Arumov with a chilling smile.

"That's what your Berezov had in mind for me," he explained. "Remember Afghan women? Their men disarmed prisoners, tied them up and gave them to the women. Remember that?"

Arumov didn't reply.

"Do you remember or not?" shouted Mironov with force that made Grishin shudder.

Arumov nodded slightly and groaned, the movement causing agonizing pain.

"Good," continued Mironov, his voice now quiet and pained. "So you recall how we found our boys later, half-eaten by dogs, severed genitals stuffed into their mouths, charred sticks in their anuses, intestines hanging out?"

Arumov nodded, slack-jawed with mortal fear.

"Yes, you do remember," continued Mironov

with rising vehemence. "Unfortunately, so do I. Yes, and I remember what it was like to speak to their families afterwards. Your son was very lucky. He didn't suffer at all – stray bullet right through the heart. Happy one moment, dead the next. We had to put him in that sealed zinc coffin because of the hot climate. Very sorry that it can't be opened. Regulations. But he was a hero."

Arumov stared at Mironov wide-eyed.

"And meanwhile your slimy friends do deals with the enemy," resumed Mironov, hatred returning to his voice. "Drugs for mines and bullets for those who captured my men, leaving me with what I had to put inside sealed coffins."

He reached over and took hold of Arumov's intestines. Grasping almost sensuously, he pulled a little.

Arumov's face transformed into a mask of agony. An awful strangled gargle issuing from his throat, and he fainted again. Mironov tipped the rest of the bucket over his head and waited, wiping his forehead with the back of the other hand.

When Arumov's eyes opened, they were unfocussed and glazed. Mironov stood well back from his victim until the glazed look sharpened.

"Here we are," he affirmed gravely. "Justice has

caught up with you at long last – but I am offering an escape."

Arumov nodded furiously, wincing with pain at the movement.

"I want a list of Berezov's assets, addresses and account numbers," Mironov told him. "If you cough up, we will give you morphine and a clean end. You can escape what you really deserve."

"What guarantee do I get?" asked Arumov in a halting stutter.

"Just one," replied Mironov. "I give you my word of honour as a Russian officer. You never had any honour, so I don't expect you to understand how iron-clad that pledge is. In any case, it's the only guarantee I offer."

For a man eviscerated with a combat knife Arumov performed a remarkably fast calculation.

"How do you know I will say anything worthwhile?" he demanded hoarsely.

"I was coming to that," replied Mironov evenly. "We have men stationed all over Moscow. If you talk fast enough, we can verify your information at random. If you aren't lying, we give you morphine, and you dream your way to the next world. But Allah help you if you lie – and you would require divine help."

Arumov nodded assent, and Mironov stepped back. A former medic from their unit gently lowered Arumov to the ground onto a stretcher lined with a foil blanket against the cold and wrapped the edges of the foil over Arumov's gaping abdomen with infinite care.

He then inserted an intravenous cannula into Arumov's forearm and injected a small amount of morphine, flushing it with saline from a bag he hung from the hoist. Next the medic cut open the expensive striped trousers and slid a urinary catheter into the man's penis, relieving a full bladder.

As morphine took its calming effect, Arumov spilled Berezov's secrets in a halting, drug-slurred voice. Grishin meticulously took down the details, and two other men periodically rushed out to make hurried calls to the scouts in relevant suburbs. A third opened a small laptop and tapped on it furiously, verifying a few banking details.

After some forty minutes Arumov stopped. Grishin, who was receiving feedback from scouts, looked up at Mironov and nodded affirmatively. Mironov finished washing his hands in water poured from a canister, picked up his suitcase and left, making a contemptuous gesture with his wet hand towards Arumov.

The medic stepped forward and knelt next to the stretcher. He drew up the contents of eight small ampoules into one syringe and injected the lot into the near-empty bag of saline above Arumov. He then opened the flow to full.

Arumov shuddered slightly, and his body relaxed in a manner entirely out of keeping with his horrific injury. His head lolled to the side, eyes closing slowly. Breathing became erratic and ceased altogether a few minutes later. The medic waited a little longer and checked for a pulse at the neck. There was none.

The stretcher was then removed to the yard and loaded into a van, which sped out of town.

***

Mironov returned to the dacha in the early hours of the morning and tiptoed to the shower, where he stood under hot water for a very long time.

He dressed in a clean track suit and entered the bedroom he occupied with Nina, lying down on the rug in front of the fire like a faithful guard dog. He fell asleep as he listened to the crackle of logs and Nina's quiet breathing coming from the bed.

A few minutes later Nina said something incoherent and sobbed without awaking, and Mironov sat bolt-upright, his hand on the butt of his pistol.

As sleep left him entirely he slowly perceived the dismal irrelevance of his weapon to Nina's well-being. Fingers slid away from the once-reassuring metal, and Mironov lay back, no longer sure of anything in this life or the next.

***

Berezov was lost in thought, staring at the snow-covered landscape rushing past the limousine in moonlight. His mistress had nodded off, assisted by the champagne she consumed at yet another of interminable parties Berezov patiently suffered at this time of year.

It was something he accepted as a necessary evil, part of being one of the larger scavengers feasting on the corpse of the communist experiment. He attended these occasions benignly, attempting to salvage what little one could by zeroing in on the slower drinkers and pumping them for their impressions of new reality. It wasn't that Berezov didn't trust his own powers of analysis – the fact was, however, that even imagining the present Russia would have a man locked up by any competent psychiatrist only years before.

Judging by the state of his mistress, further entertainment was out of the question for the evening, and Berezov was now hoping to receive some attention by morning at the earliest. This was becoming something of a habit with her, and he was growing disappointed with the return on the investment he had made in the little minx.

It was her very lucky day when they met. But for that totally random event, the lady would now be selling herself for a fraction of what he spent on her desires.

She was a bookkeeper in a large warehouse he acquired for a very different purpose to its original use, that of storing antique furniture. The former owner, nevertheless, made good money buying priceless heirlooms from desperate pensioners who sold them as little more than firewood. The furniture was restored to a presentable state and on-sold to European buyers with an average return of nine hundred percent.

But the owner ran into a dispute over *krysha,* refusing to accommodate a demand for more protection money. On the run from heavily armed people who wanted to kill him, brutally, as a lesson to others, the owner made a hasty offer. Berezov paid up and helped the owner hide with his family at some very far destination. New Zealand, from memory, wherever that may be.

He met the raven-haired beauty whilst studying the affairs of the furniture business. She did not hesitate to ditch her previous boyfriend, a mere local musician, to insinuate her perfect body into Berezov's bed. She had behaved well until now, only occasionally branching out with younger men. Berezov knew and accepted her infidelity with equanimity. There was never any illusion of love, and at his age he no longer cared about sexually transmitted diseases. Indeed he would now be proud to contract one.

They turned off the main road and slowly drove

down a snow-bound lane towards his mansion through virgin forest. Each day the lane was groomed by a bulldozer which compacted the snow, allowing pampered Western vehicles to traverse it with relative safety. Two Jeeps packed with body guards maintained their distance, one in front and one behind Berezov's car.

Berezov began to relax as they approached the destination, each journey he made in recent weeks representing a small but significant risk to his life. He was almost asleep when the car jerked hard and slid to a ragged halt across the lane.

He instantly came awake and saw that his driver had managed to escape a collision with the back of the leading Jeep, which lost control during sudden braking and ploughed into the snowdrift at the side of the road. The chauffeur was breathing a sigh of relief, having avoided blame for an expensive incident thanks to superb reflexes and German technology.

Guards spilled out of the Jeep, fanning out with weapons drawn. Berezov snapped his fingers, and the chauffeur passed him a hand-held radio.

"What is going on, in God's name?" asked Berezov harshly.

"Uh, it's here at the front..." crackled the reply. "General, you better take a look for yourself."

Without a slightest trace of rancour at having to trudge through snow in his suit and low-cut leather shoes, Berezov opened the door and marched past the Jeep, pistol in hand. He stopped suddenly, mouth open with horror.

In the middle of the road there was a crude tripod of three fir saplings, driven into the snow and tied at the top. Arumov's stark-naked body was lashed to this obscene imitation of a Christmas tree by the neck, facing the direction from which they had just arrived. The latter told him, in no uncertain manner, that the perpetrators were familiar with Berezov's movements.

The general stared at the body for a while, his gaze lingering on the squirm of intestines hanging from a long gash in the stomach. He understood the reference implied by this wound very well, and he was now entirely oblivious to the horror of the scene, scenarios rapidly turning over in his mind.

Berezov's deliberations were interrupted by the sound of forceful retching. He turned to see his mistress kneeling over the front bumper of the Jeep, heaving canapés and champagne into the snow.

The implications were instantly obvious. Berezov knew that whatever was in Arumov's head was now compromised information, and that Mironov intended it to be known.

Berezov returned to the limousine and picked up the phone to issue a string of orders.

Their effect was to triple the protection at all his local sites and put them on a full-scale military footing, telling them to expect and to be prepared for anything, from a commando assault to an air strike.

The ghost commander would now have to work for his money.

***

Mironov intended for that to happen as well. He was not at all in a hurry to attack, knowing that a constant state of alert fatigues the enemy more than actual battle. He knew that there is an economic cost as well, and an enemy that spent a long time in a state of armed anticipation is likely to be even more demoralized when the attack finally comes from nowhere and succeeds.

His men were busy arming and training, the unit still swelling from a trickle of veterans from other units who had unsettled scores from their time in uniform. Besides, the holiday season pretty much put an end to any meaningful operations. It was as good a time as any to attend to other duties.

On the cold and bleak morning of New Year's Eve Grishin drove to one of the newer suburbs of Moscow, a maze of tall concrete rectangles in which thousands of ordinary Russians eked out a living in tiny flats with uncertain amenities.

Mironov sat in the back of the car, staring at buildings that were going up just as he left for Afghanistan. There was minimal activity around the streets, in keeping with the mood of quiet despair that afflicted all honest citizens of the former Soviet colossus.

After a little back-tracking Grishin found the right building and parked, throwing a few empty rifle cartridges over the dashboard as an unsubtle warning to any who may experience more than a passing interest in the vehicle.

"One thing," said Mironov suddenly.

Grishin turned off the ignition and faced his passenger, indicating complete attention.

"That computer boy," Mironov continued. "Your nephew."

"Slava's nephew," corrected Grishin. "But go on."

"We need to do some business with him," said Mironov. "The addresses of our men were very easily found in government records. We need to stir up some mud."

Grishin nodded thoughtfully. He wrote something in a small notebook he carried in his wallet.

They emerged into the snow, then Grishin leaned down to extract a flat pocket-sized bottle of vodka from his pocket. He unscrewed the cap and took a generous swig, passing the rest to Mironov, who shook his head resolutely.

"New times dictate new conventions, Major," said Grishin firmly, holding out the bottle between them. "If you didn't need a drink before you went in... It means you don't care."

Mironov appraised the statement and nodded in acquiescence. He took a small slug and splashed a bit more around his collar for extra smell, wincing from the burn of the liquor. He returned the bottle; Grishin capped it and stuffed it into his side pocket.

They marched into the building, Grishin carrying a small briefcase filled with US dollars, the sole currency universally respected in Russia at that time. Arumov's information concerning the bank accounts he controlled was immediately verified and the money moved.

To that end they raided a computer shop where one of Grishin's men expertly deactivated the alarms. He had installed them some weeks before – but the owner refused to pay for work done, citing bogus quality concerns.

When the alarm company manager paid a visit he found the owner at the back of his establishment, sharing a bottle of vodka and a roll of spicy sausage with two local policemen. Also present was a large man in a black leather coat who did not exert himself to make introductions, busy as he was showing off his modified assault rifle to the policemen.

A few stacks of dollars next to the policemen's plates completed the picture of a mafia-sponsored operation that practised classic trickle-down economics with local law enforcement.

There was no point in getting killed over bad debts, as the manager of the alarm company understood very well. He left empty-handed but bitterly complained to his men, knowing that at least one of them would give word about how to bypass the installation, to someone or other keen to take advantage of such knowledge.

Mironov's men got there first. They set up a protective perimeter whilst someone's nephew was delivered into the darkened shop by armed escort. He turned on one of the machines permanently connected to the Internet for delectation of prospective computer buyers, and he guessed the inconsequential password within minutes.

Over the next half-hour he was busy logging onto various bank sites around the world to transfer money controlled by Arumov directly into a Nauru account Grishin set up a week before. Mironov couldn't remember the location of Nauru, but later he was happy to hear that the account was emptied into a shady bank in Moscow by morning, and the money was withdrawn as cash later that day, its trans-global trip being thereby completed to his satisfaction.

Grishin explained to Mironov that all Internet-based transactions are traceable, users being assigned temporary or permanent numeric identifiers, which Internet providers could then trace to the identity of an actual user. It was possible to use the Internet anonymously in some public places, but there were very few of them in Moscow. They were mostly frequented by teenagers, and a man of Grishin's stature would be likely to leave a lasting impression on passers-by.

The revelation that the Internet is not entirely unregulated did much to assuage Mironov's puzzlement as to why any government could tolerate such a phenomenon, and he watched with vague approval as the nephew finished his work and wiped the computer clean of any information. He then took off the latex gloves he wore as a precaution, shook hands with Mironov, hugged Grishin and was escorted home.

The doors of the shop were left open and hinges jammed – the place would be picked clean shortly after dawn by quick-witted passers-by. With any luck this would force the scoundrel owner to flee his creditors, thereby moving far enough to escape an acquaintance with Berezov's thugs once they did the inevitable homework. He deserved something bad, thought Mironov, but not that bad.

Now Grishin and Mironov stood in a rattling lift winding its way to the fifteenth floor of an apartment block with a small fraction of that money. Both wore dress uniforms.

As the lift slid to a halt Grishin downed the last of the vodka and dropped the bottle into the lift well. They marched to a distant door with faded brass numerals and checked the name on the doorbell. Hesitant sounds of a piano sonata were audible through the door.

Grishin rang the bell, a long, solitary ring which sounded harshly through the landing.

The piano fell silent, and the door was shortly opened by a blond teenager with gold-rimmed glasses, which emphasized his soft-handsome looks. Mironov's heart skipped a beat – the face staring at him from a mop of curls was the spitting image of his former corporal.

"Is Mrs Komarov home, young man?" asked Grishin benignly. He let the lapels of his coat fall away from his chest slightly, allowing the young man to see a breast full of ribbons.

"Certainly," replied the youth politely. "Let me take your coats."

He deposited the latter on the clothes horse that stands sentry at the door in every Russian home. Both men retained their shoes, carefully wiped upon entry, as befits privileged visitors.

They were led through a small apartment into the kitchen, where an ageing woman in a faded apron was toiling over a large pot of soup. A small television in the corner displayed a figure skating contest. The Russians, who once reigned supreme in that sport, were losing the tournament to Americans coached by a Russian.

The woman looked up at them with fear, but the sight of military uniforms reassured her at once. She came towards them, dropping a large spoon into the sink.

"Who are you?" she asked without belligerence.

"Mrs Komarov," replied Mironov stepping forward. "I was privileged to be your husband's last commanding officer. It is my duty to pay a visit to his family, and I now come to fulfil that duty. Forgive me for not being able to do it sooner."

"But that was over fifteen years ago," whispered the woman, large tears beginning to form in her eyes. "Surely the state could show a little decency and leave me be with my grief?"

"We do not come on behalf of any bureaucracy," replied Grishin. "The Major was himself a casualty of the same battle, and he is only now able to present his condolences in person."

The woman nodded in comprehension, wiping away her tears.

"I see," she replied breathlessly. "I am sorry, that was rude of me."

"I would react the same way," said Mironov, bowing his head slightly. "Is it possible to sit down?"

At that point the spell broke, and the startled widow was displaced by the officious mistress of a Russian home. She marched her visitors into the cramped lounge, where her son stared at a music sheet whilst straining to catch the gist of their conversation.

When they entered he stood up from the piano abruptly, awkwardly closing the instrument in an attempt to conceal his agitation. He began to leave, but Grishin raised his hand to signal that his presence is also required.

His mother darted back into the kitchen, returning with a bottle of ice-cold vodka and a few snacks, which she placed on the table in the lounge.

Grishin poured a generous quantity into each glass, exchanging a forceful glance with Mironov, who accepted defeat at that exchange and stood up with a glass in hand.

As if suddenly remembering something, the young man reached over towards the centre of the table, where a packet of cigarettes lay next to an ornate metal ashtray on a small tripod. He extracted a cheap plastic lighter from beneath the ashtray and darted to the bookshelf crammed with Russian classics, published in less turbulent times before his birth. There he lit a small candle in front of his father's portrait and returned to the table.

Mironov's hand trembled so much that he had to return the brimming tumbler to the table. Staring at the portrait, he locked eyes with the first man from his past who looked precisely as Mironov remembered, for he and Corporal Komarov had died on the same day. The face that stared at him was the same as he saw on his last morning, yet the cheap photograph had faded with age, turning the green of his best gunner's eyes pale grey.

Mironov regained control of himself, picked up his glass and raised a toast to the portrait.

"Eternal memory."

They drank, a single tear running down Grishin's face. Komarov's wife nodded sadly but remained composed. It was, after all, over fifteen years ago.

"He was a good man, your husband," Mironov told her gently.

She smiled, her still-beautiful face aflame with a sudden radiance that eclipsed sorrow.

"You are supposed to say that, I know."

"No, I mean it. Your husband was a good man,

and I was privileged to be his commander. He made a few mistakes for which he was disciplined when he first joined our unit, but none of us knew how to handle that hell to begin with."

"So what happened when he was killed?" asked his son suddenly. "I know what is written, but I don't believe anything I read."

"That's unfortunate," replied Mironov ominously. "Well, my friend, here's what happened. My unit was ordered into a very dangerous area where we were attacked with overwhelming force. Your father died trying to save what was left of my command. Most of us were killed that day."

"Why were you ordered to do something like that?"

"That's what happens in wars, son," replied Grishin, trying to pre-empt Mironov's reply. "People are ordered to do very dangerous things, and sometimes they don't survive when they fulfil their orders."

"That's just inhuman."

"Perhaps. But that's what we did in our youth, and if your generation thinks it stupid and resolves not to repeat our mistakes, what we did is already worth the sacrifice."

Mironov opened his mouth to speak but shut it firmly again. Grishin poured some more vodka.

"To all who died that day," he said gently. "May they find rest in the earth they fought for."

They brought their glasses together, and Mironov gulped the contents of his with something that could be mistaken for urgency.

"So how did my father die?" asked the youth persistently.

"In an explosion which destroyed his tank," replied Mironov, frowning. "It was fast, and I don't know any other details. I was burning in another machine when that happened."

"Were you badly injured yourself?"

"I am afraid so. I... would rather not go into it."

"That's enough, Volodya," retorted the mother firmly. "These men are not government lackeys. They came here to discharge a debt of personal honour. I hope that you will have their courage and their sense of duty if you become an officer."

The look in her son's eyes was one of abject contempt, and she pursed her lips with anger.

"I don't know where you get your ideas," she

scorned. "Your father and his comrades were only human beings in an impossible situation. They didn't have any choice, you know."

"They could have run away. Afghanistan was a wild country, and they could have made their way to the West."

"Some tried," replied Grishin sadly. "A few even survived. But you know, that's the thing about loving your country. It may be the worst in the world, but a man only ever gets one motherland, and you can't run away from that."

"I could if I had to. In fact, I'd rather leave anyway. I am not serving in the army."

Mironov and Grishin exchanged glances.

"That is a choice one has to make, young man," replied Mironov heavily. "Do you fight for your Motherland, so one day there will be no need to run away from it, or do you find a better place to live and pretend that it is yours?"

"But is that what my father was doing? Fighting for Motherland?"

"Yes."

"So how is it better for what he did?"

"He defended our unit. He saved a few of us, and we are here today."

"And what good are you to my country now?"

"What good are patriotic men in uniform?" Mironov broke into the conversation with a dangerous smile. "Oh, my young friend, you will surely witness that in your lifetime."

The youth stared at him with reproof.

"I know it is hard to have faith sometimes," continued Mironov, his voice hardening into steel. "Yes, I know that at the moment it might look as if there is no right or wrong."

The youth sneered.

"It is not hard to so conclude looking around you today. But one day there will be justice, and on that day order will be restored. There will be no more murderers on the streets, and it is the army that will make it happen."

"That's ironic, don't you think? Murderers out of uniform being killed by murderers in uniform on orders of murderers in the Kremlin?"

"Perhaps. But that is where murderers belong, my friend. In uniform and in the Kremlin. They do not belong on the streets."

Everyone looked at Mironov in surprise, but his expression was serene as he told them what he alone knew on this miserable earth.

"There always were murderers," he explained sadly and quietly. "That is why we invented uniforms and why we built the Kremlin. That is in the natural order of things – it is possible for life to go on that way. When murderers roam the streets amongst innocent and defenceless people – life, as we generally understand it, stops. Which is where we are now."

"I am not sure I follow," said Komarov junior, bellicosity leaving his voice.

"That's probably a good sign," replied Mironov. "But remember what I told you, and one day it will make sense. Anyway, there is something else we need to discuss."

He faced the youth's mother.

"Your family has made its share of sacrifices," he said firmly. "We want you to take this."

She took the briefcase and nodded uncertainly.

"Open it."

She struggled a little with a rusty clasp but eventually prized it open and looked at the contents, her eyes going wide.

"What am I supposed to do with this?"

"Volodya, for one thing. Get him out of here before his eighteenth birthday. He is not to be conscripted."

She nodded, biting her lips.

Grishin wrote something in his notebook, tore off a sheet and handed it to her.

"This man is going to contact you in the next few days or you will report him to me," he said briskly. "He runs an introduction agency to marry Russian women to well-off foreigners, and he owes me many favours."

She smiled briefly through brimming tears and shook her head. Grishin ignored her reaction.

"He is going to find you a way to obtain residency some place decent and safe, and you will both go there. Your son will not survive five minutes in the army," he told her gently. "You can obtain false medical exemptions, but that method is not fully reliable."

She began to cry, hiding her face in her hands.

"They are sending young conscripts to yet

another war," said Mironov. "But not like ours. In our time professionals were in charge, and now they are not. It's a meat grinder, and no one seems to care that they are sending young boys against hardened troops. It takes a very different man to serve now, and your son is not such a man."

She nodded, without raising her head. Her son stood up and knelt next to his mother, placing an arm around her shoulders.

"They are right," he told her briefly. "I have to get out of here. But you really should come with me."

"Please think about it," said Mironov as he rose from the table. "I was unable to preserve the life of my corporal, and there is nothing that I won't do to preserve the life of his son."

***

As streets filled with last-minute shoppers rushing to top up stocks for New Year's Eve, Mironov and Grishin were speeding towards their final destination of the day, the Lefkovich household.

Grishin told him that Lefkovich had died a few years before, of cancer that left him paralysed for the last few months of his life. He did not lose his superb Jewish humour, being a great companion to old comrades who took turns to help with his care.

Mironov inquired whether anyone contributed to the cancer by refusing appropriate medical help, but Grishin firmly stated that the condition was inoperable. Money, however, was a problem in the last few years of the late sergeant's life. His sons emigrated to Israel, but the youngest was promptly put in jail for a drunken car accident, and the elder brother was saddled with feeding two families.

They parked at yet another grimy curb and crossed a busy road, dodging dirty slush from hurtling traffic. They started scaling the stairs of an older apartment block where Lefkovich had lived since returning from the war.

He had served for another year, then ended up with a medical discharge, after spending five months in a burns unit. He had been helping to offload wounded men onto a transport helicopter when an accurately aimed missile hit the machine through open cargo doors, blowing everything in sight to shreds. Lefkovich was sheltered from the blast behind a *BTR*, but the spreading pool of burning aviation fuel enveloped him from all sides. He climbed on top of the armoured personnel carrier, but it too caught fire. Lefkovich was lucky to escape with his life.

As they neared the third floor they heard a commotion and stopped in alarm. An older woman was shouting at someone, then she screamed and fell silent. There was a harsh male voice, then a lot of noise suggesting furniture movement.

Grishin recognized the woman's voice, and they ran up the remainder of the stairs in time to see three large men heft a handsome antique desk out of the flat.

"As you were," shouted Grishin, his voice trembling with fury. He pointed his pistol at the men, and Mironov did likewise. "What is this outrage? How dare you harass a veteran's widow?"

"Hey, general," replied one of the men curtly. "We are just earning a living, all right?"

An older woman hobbled through the door, nursing a bruise on her cheekbone.

"Ah, Grishin," she greeted him sadly. "You've come in time for the show. It seems that I owe these gentlemen some money for the funeral. They couldn't wait for me to sell this stuff properly."

"Which one of you hit her?" asked Mironov, raising his pistol.

There was no response.

"Tell me now or I will kill you all!," roared Mironov, a savage expression spreading over his face. The men put down the desk, but they faced him without fear.

"So I did," replied the man closest to him. "Put down that pistol, *soldatik* – let's see how brave you really are, man on man."

Mironov stared at him for a few seconds and nodded. He safed the pistol and tossed it to Grishin, who caught it deftly.

The return movement was too fast to see, the gloved fist catching his opponent mid-face to demolish the nose. Only a split second later Mironov's knee hammered into the man's groin, felling him to the floor.

"Put that desk back where you found it," Mironov ordered the others. "Very carefully."

He lifted his victim off the floor by the lapels of his jacket as if the larger man was a sack of hay.

The victim managed to remain on his feet, gulping air and nearly blind from streaming tears, a result of a ragged break in his nose.

Mironov shook very hard, slamming the man's head into the wall. He did this repeatedly, then pivoted on his heels and threw the rag-like body down the flight of stairs. The man came to rest at the next landing, where he lay moaning.

The other debt collectors emerged from the door and went past Mironov gingerly, pressing their backs to the wall.

"Collect your garbage and leave," spat Mironov, pointing down the stairs. "Never come near this lady again. She is protected zone. Understood?"

"Yes, general," replied one of the men eagerly. They ran down the stairs and hefted their colleague, making their way out of the building with all possible speed.

Mironov and Grishin came inside, to be assailed by the stench of old cooking fat. The flat had low ceilings, scuffed wooden floors and a multitude of other stale smells, but its furniture spoke of a different fortune. Lefkovich was the son of an aeronautical engineer who met his end in the prison camps after the Great War. Being sired by "an enemy of the people", Lefkovich was denied tertiary education, ending up as an infantry private instead. He quickly found his way to the paratroops, where his lightning-fast intelligence soon made him a rare master of diversion techniques, and it was only a matter of time before he and Mironov found themselves on the same air base, being trained in Farsi language and Iranian culture.

Mironov removed his coat and placed it on the stand along with his peaked hat. Grishin shut the front door.

The widow emerged from the bathroom, rubbing her tender cheek. She smelled of medicinal lineament.

"This was our commanding officer in *Afgan*, Natalya Fedorovna," Grishin told her brightly. "Major Vitya came to pay his respects."

She squinted at Mironov in the dim light of the vestibule.

"Viktor Mironov?" she asked incredulously. "But I was told you died!"

"That was believed to be correct at the time," replied Mironov woodenly.

The woman nodded knowingly. She was of a vintage that saw absolute truths rewritten by each generation.

"Sit down, boys," she said with a trace of fatigue

in her voice. "I don't have much to offer, so I hope you don't mind some plain tea."

"Perfect, Natalya Fedorovna," replied Grishin, patting her on the shoulder. "Don't mind us, we will get our fill soon enough."

She nodded and sighed sadly, thinking of the lonely New Year's Eve that was bearing down on her very fast. She made no plans to join another family, and her celebration was to be hollow indeed. She was still hoping that both sons would remember to call her from Israel, but their track record left a lot to be desired.

Grishin guessed her thoughts and followed her into the kitchen.

"Why don't you leave, at long last?" he asked the elderly woman.

He knew that she had resisted the ravages of her life until her husband's death – then the ill effects of living through the most outrageous period of Russian history caught up with her rapidly, turning her short hair white and her figure skeletal.

She did not at all dismiss Grishin's question. It was not, of course, a new train of thought – but such was her consternation that she welcomed an opportunity to restate her arguments.

"It's so daunting," she replied with fatigue. "I have my flat, my friends, my books, the theatres... In Israel I will have a closet in my son's apartment and a leaking shower to contend with. Look, I've been there, and that's enough. It is better to be miserable in a place I know than in a place I don't."

"But if you got sick..." suggested Grishin.

"Then I will go," she replied shortly. "But I am not, for now. God willing, I will die suddenly and save everyone a lot of trouble."

Grishin only shook his head in disapproval, helping her carry the tea glasses and the kettle to the lounge, where Mironov sat at the table. He stared at yet another portrait – one of an older man with drooping moustache and a powerfully hooked nose. A man who had survived an abattoir in Afghanistan and grew old because of Mironov's action, to die of an old man's disease. Old enough, at any rate – few Russian men were now surviving to their seventieth birthday.

He accepted his tea with a vacant expression of thanks, watching the old woman fuss around the lounge.

"Did he ever talk about our final battle?" he asked suddenly. The banter between Grishin and the old woman ceased as she stopped to think it over.

"Only once," she replied. "He didn't like talking about the war. But one day our second son entered the army in Israel. He asked his father for advice, and it was then that Itzik suddenly talked about you. He told him everything. That was my commanding officer, he told our boy. I hope you die like he did if your time comes."

Mironov sat still for a while, then nodded grimly.

"Very well, he said neutrally. "We now need to discuss your needs."

The old woman smiled sadly.

"I have many and I have none," she reported. "Surely you won't send someone to help me queue for toilet paper every week. It's an awful thing, you know – when shops run out of toilet paper. There is nothing good in the newspapers these days, so I really resent buying them. At least in the old Soviet times you could read something amusing as you prepared the newspaper for proper use."

Both men grinned.

"We will send someone to buy you a roll every day if we must," replied Mironov. "Anything else?"

"Oh, money, I suppose," she said with a heavy sigh. "It's impossible to survive on my pension, even on double what they pay me. When they pay me."

Mironov turned to Grishin, who wrote a few words in his notebook and nodded to indicate that the task would be performed without further prompting.

The offer was open-ended. Mironov set a tidy percentage of Arumov's funds aside for the families of his former command. Even so, his was not a substantial undertaking, given the likely lifespan of someone with Natalya Fedorovna's prospects in life.

"Don't sell anything," Grishin told her, looking around the lounge room. "If anyone demands money, give them this and tell them to call me if they value their life."

He handed over a business card with a mobile number scrawled across the lower margin.

She stood up and placed it in a mother-of-pearl box in which she clearly kept her valuables.

"You are a kind ghost," she said to Mironov with a smile, and he instantly realized that she knew the entire story of his reappearance. That was no surprise – there were plenty of rumours on the streets, most of them growing wilder at each retelling. This was all to be encouraged.

"A ghost must be true to his purpose," he replied

with a rare smile creasing his grim face. "Your husband tried to save my life at the expense of his. It is not something I could forget."

"Vitya," she said gently, looking at him with concern. "Major Vitya... I get an impression of an unbreakable man with a rigid moral code."

"All of that is correct," said Grishin.

"No, it is not," she turned to Mironov with sudden vehemence. "Nobody is unbreakable, understand? It is so cruel, plunging a man like you into our present reality. Whoever put you on ice and let you loose now must verily be a servant of Satan."

"Who knows," said Mironov with a chuckle. "But be assured that I am not."

"So you came back to kill the ones responsible?"

"Every single one of them."

She nodded. "And anyone who gets in the way?"

"That is not in doubt either."

"And what then?"

Mironov stopped short, startled by the question. It was something he had completely failed to consider.

"It doesn't matter," he answered after a long pause.

"But it does," said Natalya Fedorovna. "Fool, you were sacred to your men. Now you come back from the dead, whatever that is – and will you subject them to your death all over again?"

"I...don't have any plans to die," replied Mironov slowly. "It is not as if I intend on self-destruction at the end of my mission."

"The mission. Are you planning to survive it?"

"Surely."

"Then it is your duty to begin a real life afterwards. Do you hear?"

Mironov opened his mouth to speak, then closed it again, thinking of an appalling prospect of life after uniform.

"I know you don't understand what such a life is," said the old woman forcefully, placing her gnarled hand over his. She stared into his eyes as if to transmit her great will, and Mironov nodded involuntarily.

"You owe it to your men, as old and as stupid as

they may be now," she went on. "You are to set an example, understand?"

Mironov thought momentarily and slowly nodded his agreement.

"Whatever real life means," he promised. "I will make it my next mission. I will award myself that one privilege – to decide what my final mission should be about."

***

They said goodbye to the old woman and emerged from the dingy apartment block onto the street, to find a few suspicious-looking youths hanging around their car with evident ill intent. As soon as the youths saw them, they melted into the landscape with speed.

Grishin walked all the way around the car to check that nothing was untoward – in that dismal era cars were often relieved of their wheels and left on blocks of wood. The blocks were not provided out of kindness, but to allow a retrieval of the thieves' jack.

They drove around a few streets looking for a tail but were soon certain that they were not being followed. Grishin then drove to a prearranged rendezvous where Nina stood on a corner in a demure woollen overcoat.

Mironov got out and opened the door for her, and she nodded her thanks in silence. He could smell the alcohol on her breath, and even though she tried to turn away, the sparse rays of the setting winter sun made tear tracks glisten on her cheeks.

Mironov got into the back seat after her, Grishin pulling away from the kerb smoothly.

"Is everything under control?" he asked carefully. There was clearly no point in asking whether everything was all right.

She nodded tersely, looking straight ahead.

They drove out of Moscow and back to the villa, where a quiet celebration was under way. A few men who lived locally had gone back to their families, but the rest joined Mironov from all over the expanse of Russia, and they were making the most of an opportunity to spend New Year's Eve with their old comrades.

Nina did not join them, returning straight to her room. She locked herself in the bathroom and emerged an hour later, going to bed immediately. When Mironov came by, she turned away and pulled the blanket over her head. He knelt next to the bed for a while, then turned off the light and left.

It was his first New Year's Eve in Russia since his aunt's party, but he felt very little beside poignancy. In truth, he realized, he was now emotionally fatigued to the point of numbness.

It took every ounce of his will to stay with the others until midnight. Champagne was drunk, last toasts were pronounced, and the old soldiers returned to their rooms, now protected by a ring of sentries scattered around the outbuildings of the forest mansion.

By now their presence was likely to be general knowledge amongst locals, who frequently ventured into the woods on skis. There were no illusions about the speed with which the enemy could get hold of this information, and alternative arrangements were being made.

Mironov went back to his room and took a long shower to cleanse himself from the tasks of the departed day.

When he emerged and padded towards the fire, Nina called out softly. He turned around and approached her bed.

Wordlessly, she turned aside the blanket and stretched out her hand towards him. He sat down on the bed instead, taking a deep breath in.

"Don't say anything," she said hoarsely.

He nodded and climbed into bed, lying there awkwardly until she rolled against him and put her head on his shoulder. He felt her tears on his skin.

"It's impossible to bear," she whispered. "Any of it."

He opened his mouth to ask, but she put a soft hand over his face and held him harder. He reached out to return the embrace.

Her breathing gradually levelled out to a calmer rhythm, and he felt the strength ebb from her grasp.

He gently freed his arm and placed it over her cheek, feeling its warm dampness.

Nina sighed and said something softly in her sleep, then Mironov let the tension drain from his body and lay quietly in the darkness, awaiting the mercy of exhausted sleep.

**

After long deliberations the choice of target fell on what appeared to be a major linchpin of Berezov's operations, a large brick warehouse built in the middle of a now abandoned railway yard. It was a low windowless building covering a few hectares. Judging by its soot-stained appearance, it saw a lot of traffic when steam still ruled the vast distance of the Russian hinterland.

The building was chosen by someone who contemplated potential enemies at length. It was surrounded by an expanse of wide-open ground criss-crossed with ditches and ice-bound tracks. It could not be approached at speed on foot and not at all by car.

The only vehicle access was through a series of rail crossings, a path that wound through open ground laboriously. Its bends could not be negotiated at speed, meaning that an assault vehicle would suffer withering fire before it got near the warehouse. There were many sandbagged silhouettes on the roof, each a multiple machine gun emplacement.

An old freight car was derailed near the entrance, forcing vehicles to make three tight turns on the final approach to the gate. It prevented any vehicle that did make it that far from ramming the roller door at speed.

There was also a rear exit, a smaller roller door

that never opened. It appeared to be too narrow to serve any real purpose, but could be a potential escape route for the defendants. The plan stipulated that none should escape.

Whenever the main door opened a security detail would emerge on foot and fan around the area, positioning themselves behind the metal debris.

They looked disciplined and well-armed, probably freshly demobilized paratroopers who were being pushed out of the Red Army in the early days after the putsch – elite units once massed on the border in East Germany. Used to the best living conditions available in the Eastern Bloc, these soldiers and their families were hastily repatriated and housed in tents pitched on parade grounds in the middle of winter.

When these units were disbanded, usually to make room for real estate development, the men were informally asked to take their equipment with them. That saved foreign project managers the worry of working around old munitions and resulted in an influx of highly trained and well-armed men into mafia ranks. They plied their trade by fighting military-style engagements on city streets.

One foreign car maker distinguished itself by hiring a band of such ex-soldiers in response to demands for protection money. A new showroom was duly opened despite threats, but not before a frontal assault by a mafia unit was repelled with small arms fire and the odd rocket-propelled grenade. The battle raged in the middle of a working day, less than ten kilometres away from the Kremlin.

Fortunately, the assault was poorly prepared and resulted in no casualties or major damage. Except, possibly, a few brain cells as the leader of democratic Russia drank to the soldiers' health upon hearing the shots. It was as productive an official response as anyone expected at that time.

In contrast, Mironov's operation boasted elegant and deadly simplicity.

Three squads penetrated the yard immediately after nightfall, fanning out to cover the rear approach to the warehouse. They crawled along the ground very slowly, camouflaged with white bedsheets. They carried light machine guns and boxes of ammunition fitted with large rubber wheels that once belonged to furniture trolleys. That made them easier and quieter to haul along broken ground whilst crawling.

They made slow progress to within three hundred meters of the building, two squads setting up firing positions to catch any reinforcements which may arrive in their sector. The third squad was positioned to mop up anyone running from the rear entrance of the warehouse.

The main assault team arrived from the other direction by rail. If Grishin had any doubts about the persona of his commander, they evaporated right there and then – it was just like Mironov to turn the main obstacle to his advantage with one stroke.

The rails that made it hard to attack the warehouse on foot or by armoured vehicle made it possible to approach the stationary target with armour that was every bit as effective.

They simply followed disused tracks until they joined a working trunk, and there they hijacked a slow-moving train that consisted of empty coal cars. One of Mironov's men took the place of the engine driver, who was much relieved when invited to leave intact.

Although filthy, coal cars made ideal attack vehicles, boasting steel sides that looked much thicker than any armour. They could probably be overturned if hit with sufficient force, but Mironov very much doubted that anything like heavy artillery was at hand in the warehouse.

As the train reversed around the bend that concealed it from Berezov's men, there was movement on the warehouse roof. A spotlight erratically carved pre-dawn darkness, guards unsure as to how they should react. They clearly had no means of stopping the train, and they were not prepared to leave the security of their position to challenge the driver.

They did call for help, just as Mironov anticipated, with a truckload of men arriving almost instantly. Mironov watched them drive towards the locomotive through the green haze of night vision goggles. He signalled for the attack to commence just as the tailgate of the truck dropped down, men spilling from the cavernous canvas-topped body.

A single missile streaked towards the truck, hitting it just in front of the rear axle. The vehicle exploded in a cloud of shrapnel, orange streaks reaching the façade of the warehouse and shattering the darkness. With night goggles now off, Mironov directed fire to the machine gun emplacements on the roof. Two more missiles were aimed just near the roller door, the second blasting clear through the brick wall.

Mironov waited for the wall to collapse, then ordered five missiles into the breach. They streaked inside the warehouse through darkness, and a split second later he heard the roar of a large explosion as something volatile was hit inside.

Flames soon shot through the sinking roof, their size and extent leaving Mironov with no doubt that everything inside was doomed. He picked up the radio and called the rear machine gun emplacement, to be told that no one attempted to leave in their direction.

A few cars began to zig-zag on the path to the front door, clearly panicked middle-rank commanders attempting to evaluate the situation personally. Most died within sight of the burning warehouse, only one car managing to evade a missile by skidding across the tracks, its occupants spilling from the doors and disappearing into the rail yard just as their vehicle exploded in a fireball.

When the rear exit was clearly on fire the machine gun squads left their emplacements and ran past the inferno towards the nearest coal cars. They clambered over the edges and slid inside over oblique walls, covering themselves in coal dust. The train began to roll away, gathering speed at leisure.

Not knowing the schedule of the busy line they didn't risk going onto the main trunk and left the train just short of the junction, clearing the area on foot. Their equipment and camouflage uniforms stowed in used-looking haversacks, they split up and ambled through the night streets of Moscow, dressed to resemble homeless men. A fleet of cars inconspicuously collected them at pre-arranged locations.

Mironov and Grishin were driven to the outskirts of the city in an old Lada jeep. The driver approached a row of old houses and chose a dark street corner, where he parked, nodded to his passengers and left the vehicle. He disappeared into the heavy snowfall that began to obscure the horizon. Grishin got into the driver's seat and turned around, heading out of Moscow.

They drove back to the country estate in silence, Mironov frantically engaged in mental calculations which he did not share with Grishin.

The vehicles were parked in the courtyard and camouflaged with snow-covered canvas to make them invisible to aerial surveillance. They were well past reasonable time to change locations, and Mironov stared through the snowstorm with apprehension. It rendered enemies not only impossible to hear, but near-invisible to boot.

He entered the building, peeling his coat and gloves as he approached Nina's bedroom. His gait was near-silent on the carpet runner, and he was reasonably sure she remained asleep as he closed the door behind him. He had lubricated the hinges with a squirt of gun oil the day before.

Embers still glowed in the fireplace, and Mironov knelt to add another log to the pile. It crackled as he undressed and walked into the shower, forcing himself to enjoy it at length.

He was accustomed to entering showers ahead of

a long queue of subordinates, as required by protocol. However, he valued their comfort far more than his own, and that destroyed his basic human right to enjoy a good scrub without guilt.

Mironov came back to the room wearing a gown of terry cloth he found in the shower. He lay down on the floor and stared at the flames which began to lick the fresh log. Nina continued to breathe evenly, and Mironov stretched out on the rug in front of the fire, not quite ready for sleep. The adrenaline of the railway yard was ebbing from his system none too fast.

His gaze fell on the pile of old newspapers, and he reached out to pull them towards him. He grasped the yellowing page of what was once the leading Soviet daily, looked at the date and began to read.

An hour later the log was nearly consumed, but Mironov's eyes continued to bore the old newsprint, and his hands continued to turn pages. One part of his brain kept on absorbing the material he read – as part of him applauded, part of him protested, and the rest of him mourned.

He learned of an explosion in a nuclear reactor which contaminated Northern Europe. It killed many people and would continue to kill those who lived in the vicinity. He read of men in and out of uniform who undertook suicide missions to construct a concrete sarcophagus over the remains of the leaking reactor.

That event was the first crack to appear in the edifice of the Soviet state, he learned after reading most of the pile. Freedom to speak, then freedom to trade. Freedom to ignore the state and freedom to commit crimes with total impunity, then the surreal reality in which he was becoming well-orientated. So much so, in fact, that it called his own sanity into question.

He read references to an uprising one late summer, when his brother Guards refused to fire on protesters. That decision, arrived at anonymously and amorphously, with neither a debate nor a vote by a handful of officers, ended a long, blood-soaked chapter of his country's history.

The flames lit the newsprint brightly as the next log caught fire, and Mironov continued to read. A silver-haired politician, who happened to be in the right place at the right moment, mounted a stilled tank with the right speech, thereby ensuring his role as the first leader of a new Russia. He won immense respect, but ever since he tried to wash it away with a river of vodka he poured down his peasant throat.

Mironov read about a criminal enclave in the mountains that served as a trigger for another Caucasian war, and he shook his head in wonder. In officer academy Mironov wrote a long essay on the triggers of the Caucasian war in 1830's, lasting thirty years and costing the lives of a third of the area's population, not to mention the toll on the Russian military. All without conclusive results.

Mironov served with enough natives of that region to be certain that a few cases of vodka and a few bags of money would have achieved a much better result than a mountain of corpses. He did not quite state so in his essay, but his conclusions were not well-received in the late 1960's.

At the end of that decade there were over three million men in Soviet uniform, and a third of these were as battle-worthy as their fathers who stormed Berlin. The rest were conscripts good for little more than digging up potatoes, but that could not be said of the rocket forces, who wielded the greatest nuclear arsenal in the history of the planet.

In those heady days no officer, still drunk on the Soviet triumph over the deadliest army ever assembled, could conceive that one day his thermonuclear empire would find itself stalemated by a minuscule enemy force. He wrote this only as a tantalizing theoretical possibility well beyond his imagining.

Mironov's essay attracted only a mild rebuke, implying as it did that overwhelming force was not the best tactic for Russians a century before and it would be no better now.

Even in Afghanistan ultimate failure was a remote and unlikely concept. The Soviet Army remained a total master of occupied territory, going where it wanted with near-impunity. Guerillas were able to do no more than make them pay toll.

He shook his head in annoyance as he tossed the old newspapers into the fire and pulled the rough blanket over his feet.

Mironov lay back and put his head on the kit bag filled with clothes he used as a pillow. He closed his eyes and banished all further thoughts. With dawn already creeping past the edge of the horizon, he lay still and listened to Nina's breathing.

The rhythm of that sound lulled him into the deep, dreamless sleep of one whose soul cannot accommodate further insult.

***

The warehouse had burned to the ground. Its stores of fuel, ammunition, furniture and solvents required for drug manufacture had created a firestorm which was hot enough to melt the sheet metal of sports cars. Stolen throughout Europe, these vehicles were now reduced to smooth slugs of dirty metal.

Mixed by cowering prisoners in Stalin's day, the mortar had cracked in the heat, large chunks of walls collapsing into rubble.

There was no question of finding body parts among the debris. Combustion of warehouse contents was so complete that by morning only smoking railway sleepers in the immediate vicinity of the wall were still recognizable to a careful observer.

That landscape of charred rubble confronted Berezov as he arrived just after breakfast.

Approaching the railway yard in his armoured Mercedes, Berezov felt genuine fear for his safety for the first time in many years. That was a forgotten feeling from the days when he ventured into the mountain valleys of Afghanistan.

He had fought that fear as he traded guns for crude heroin with Islamic fanatics, who saw Russians and fellow Afghans alike as sinners equally deserving of extermination.

Yes, that was the last time he had a reasonable expectation of being killed in action – rattling on his "super-secret" missions in a stinking personnel carrier, accompanied by a few low-rank accomplices who manhandled heavy munitions. If he was intercepted by a different guerilla group or found out by his own, instant death was the best possible outcome and an unlikely one at that.

Emerging from the car to study the burnt warehouse, Berezov had another deja-vu – a flashback to the moment which launched his highly successful criminal career. He was never as frightened in his life as the moment he stepped from a personnel carrier onto rocky soil.

He remembered how he casually approached a bearded man with a jewelled dagger at his belt and an assault rifle tucked behind his shoulders, knowing that within the next ten minutes he will be either very rich or very dead.

He didn't so much fear death, he recalled, as anxiety as to whether he could really pull it off – a pampered commander of imperial troops trading with a fanatical savage, both traitors to their respective sides.

In retrospect, the bearded Afghan fanatics were some of the saner – certainly the most honourable – of trading partners he had met afterwards. The Taliban wouldn't have acted like mad dogs without provocation, thought Berezov grimly, staring at the ashes of merchandise worth millions of dollars.

In the underworld scores were now settled mainly with targeted assassinations, and any property worth taking was removed, promptly and entirely. Whoever had burned the warehouse with utter contempt for its worth was totally alien to that familiar landscape.

Whilst Berezov had uneasy relationships with a number of fellow criminals on any given day, none of them were of a caliber to destroy his base. None of his known rivals could put on that superb display of tactical improvisation, not to mention a lack of material needs.

The identity of his nemesis was not, therefore, in dispute.

***

A German limousine swept through the Red Square, expensive winter tyres rattling over the cobblestones that lined the power centre of Russia for four centuries.

Collapse of communism thus achieved what Hitler's armies singularly failed to do.

A *UAZ* with a small red flag on the bonnet peeled off from the guard detachment and intercepted the Mercedes, leading it to a small alcove away from tourists and other idle observers. It entered a small courtyard behind the sprawling complex, known as the People's Palace – despite the fact that normal people only entered to clean it.

Minin and Berezov stepped out of the car. They were searched, thoroughly and rather brusquely, by four crisply uniformed guardsmen, surrounded by a circle of other soldiers whose assault rifles were not at all ceremonial. At the completion of the search they were lead into an inconspicuous doorway and boarded an old wooden lift adorned with baize carpet. They rode the lift in absolute silence, accompanied by two soldiers who avoided eye contact.

Silence was maintained as they were lead down a corridor lined with priceless paintings from centuries past, mostly portraits of imperial warriors – not a few of whom ended their lives after a walk down the same corridor.

They were ushered into a lavishly baroque waiting room, but there was no waiting. Gilded doors opened as soon as they entered, and they were led to the President's desk. They stopped just short of it, hands by their sides and bowing slightly.

The President of the Russian Federation acknowledged their presence with a drunken nod. His silver hair was perfectly coiffured, but the face beneath was a coarse, ruddy mask of a chronic alcoholic. Bloodshot eyes were narrow slits in puffy lids.

He motioned for them to sit down, Berezov craving further cues as to how drunk that sorry leader was that morning.

"S Rozhdestvom, Gospodin Prezident," said Berezov brightly, opening with a mention of the forthcoming Orthodox Christmas.

"Likewise to yourself, general," replied the President in the same tone, and with some consternation Berezov realized that the man was as sober as he had seen him for some time.

"You know Vladimir, of course," the President pointed to a lean man with a dour expression and a tall forehead beneath thin blond hair. He stood at the wall next to the President's desk, body held rigidly and awkwardly, his entire appearance signalled humourless officialdom.

The gnome, as he was known to cartoonists, jerked his chin in an expression of contempt. It was indeed an ironic scene – two older men, who had spent their lives draped in Communist Party slogans, wishing each other joy at a religious festival. Should there be any truth in that faith, conveyed the gnome's expression, both of you will spend eternity in the hottest part of hell.

"We had met," replied Berezov, now entirely uncomfortable. Rumours said that nowadays the President does no business without this runt, who rapidly rose from the middle ranks of KGB because of his talent for Byzantine machinations.

Any Roman usurper would find the gnome's skills entirely useful, and the gnome, in turn, would find the lethal intrigue of a Roman court entirely familiar.

The gnome nodded curtly, indicating that business was to be commenced.

"We come to you with a problem, *Gospodin Prezident*," commenced Berezov. "Our business operation is being subjected to an outrageous attack from an obscure group of individuals. We believe them to be disgruntled *Afgan* veterans, and there is concern that they armed themselves to mount systematic attacks against new business interests – not just ours – motivated by reactionary ideals."

The President and the gnome both performed an instant calculation. They processed Berezov's statement as input and arrived at the following output: Berezov is up against a threat he can't handle, and he is offering whatever is reasonable in return for help from state muscle.

"That is most unsettling," commented the President in his best patriotic voice. "There are many reactionaries opposing our democratic transition, and we cannot allow them to express their opposition with bullets."

"I believe that a modest detachment of battle-worthy troops will deal with this problem," ventured Minin. "It is only a matter of time before we discover their whereabouts. We know the identity of their leader, a former Guards officer, but we are unable to find the records that list those who served with him. I assume that they covered their tracks, and that they are holed up somewhere together, to avoid being dealt with by more ordinary means."

"You mean, one at a time by your own thugs," said the gnome with distaste. "That's the problem with thuggery, general – there are always bigger thugs."

"These are uncertain times," replied Berezov reasonably. "An operation like mine has to be protected by whatever means present themselves."

"These uncertain times are coming to an end," announced the gnome forcefully, staring at Berezov from beneath his tall forehead, now tilted forward aggressively. "Soon there will be no more mayhem on our streets. It is hoped that you will recognize the time to disarm when it comes."

"One would hope so indeed," replied Berezov, his tone turning hostile and hard.

Be a little more careful, said that steel ring in his voice to the gnome – in a criminal den fortune can be a fickle whore. You never know when the toes you tread on today are connected to the arse you will be forced to kiss tomorrow.

The President waved his hand, calling the proceedings to order.

"Times are indeed uncertain, Vladimir," he affirmed with a pacifying sideways glance at the gnome. "I believe that assistance is in order – I always found the general a very good man to deal with. Naturally, we would expect his cooperation with any official action, as deemed necessary."

Berezov nodded eagerly.

"There is a small matter I must discuss with you, general," said the President, reaching into his desk. The gnome rolled his eyes in irritation, seeing a bottle of vodka and two large tumblers emerge from a mahogany drawer inlaid with gold.

"Vladimir," said the President. "Be so good as to take ah... this gentleman into your office and organize something useful. I wish to speak to the general alone."

Minin hefted the large pile of documents he brought with him, smiling broadly at the gnome. He knew that once so ordered, their mutual former employer would complete the jigsaw with lightning speed.

Thirty minutes later Minin and Berezov again traversed the Red Square in their limousine. Once safely outside the palace, Berezov turned to Minin and indicated that the latter was to take down a dictation.

As they sped through Moscow Minin wrote down a list of waywardly independent members of parliament and what was to be perpetrated on each by Berezov's men.

The general had no difficulty remembering who required what, and he hoped that the president would not fail to remember that either.

***

A long troop convoy stretched along the highway, pushing in the direction specified at short notice. No one trusted anybody.

As Minin expected, gaps in his intelligence were filled instantly, reports of unexplained movements soon piling up on the relevant officer's desk.

Interrogation of locals near a defunct factory which used to manufacture anti-tank missiles, of the kind used on the warehouse, was most revealing. The foreman of the factory proved a little reticent to share information, but changed his mind after relatively minor damage.

A vehicle matching the description of a Jeep taken from Berezov's men was seen at the factory. There were also frequent sightings of that vehicle in one of the suspect locations reported, not far from the historic Sofrino estate. Aerial reconnaissance did the rest.

Some ten kilometres short of destination the convoy began to split up, maintaining strict radio silence. Detachments were deployed from different directions to surround an area of birch forest around five kilometres in diameter, spilling troops on skis from trucks, which remained well away from the action. It was uncertain whether the regiment had enough fuel to return the troops to base if these vehicles were lost.

As foot soldiers completed the encirclement manoeuvre, an armoured column drove down a forest track that displayed evidence of extensive recent traffic.

Their encirclement complete, the ring of men began to tighten around a sprawling complex of immaculate buildings, built by German prisoners of war in the forest. Firing began when they came into visual range of the dacha.

Three armoured vehicles came forward, ready to rain hell if missiles were used by the defenders, but there was only sparse automatic fire, which seemed to be poorly directed.

One armoured vehicle got close enough to the source of that fire. Seeing muzzle flashes inside an old shed, the gunner drilled it with automatic cannon, destroying the thin wooden wall entirely. As fire from within ceased, men raced from the forest on skis towards the building.

There was no one inside. It turned out that a few belt-fed machine guns were suspended from ceilings to cover all directions from the dacha. Hung from their triggers were sheets of plywood, which moved in the wind, triggering single-round fire at random. That resulted in a strange firing pattern that harmlessly went over the heads of the attackers. The aim, clearly, was to avoid loss of life whilst buying time.

It was never determined how the men escaping from the dacha avoided the encirclement – but Russians have no illusion about control over their environment.

On a table in the dining hall they found a case of vodka and a single pistol round. There was a short note to say that vodka belongs to the soldiers, and the bullet should be passed to Berezov, who may be wise to use it on himself before the sender chases him to ground. It was all radioed back to headquarters, who ordered the troops to return to base.

Whilst soldiers were doing justice to the vodka as prescribed, an ageing captain went into the trees to answer the call of nature. Once out sight he extracted a cell phone from his winter fatigues and placed a call to Minin. The news was all bad.

***

Mironov was not sorry to lose his base. Old veterans were ready to evacuate even before they received warning, and most had left by road. A few stayed behind and set up the guns, then made excellent use of a nuclear shelter that had another exit, emerging some distance into the forest.

The rearguard made their way to the highway later that day, being picked up by a few hastily summoned private vehicles. They returned to Moscow through roads checked in advance for police cordons. Mobile telephony made life very hard for police.

Their arsenal had been transferred to a location closer to Moscow even prior to the attack on the warehouse. As they were leaving the dacha, the case of vodka was the only object too heavy to evacuate at short notice. It was briefly debated whether each man should pack a bottle, but the consensus was that the brand is not that good. It was one of the new cut-price labels, probably distilled in some plant that once made antifreeze or insect repellent, from similar ingredients.

Now scattered all over Moscow, the chain of command was maintained via a network of stolen mobile telephones. The force was divided into squads of ten each, and the leader of each squad was in direct contact with Grishin, who even returned to work to avoid various rumours. Moscow underworld was now rife with whispers about an army of ghosts who were terrorizing organized crime, and it would not do to spoil these notions with facts.

Indeed, Mironov ordered his men to feed such rumours. With supernatural on his side, following up the action at the warehouse with lightning raids and assassinations was easy work.

Berezov appealed for further help from the Kremlin, but his request for an appointment was declined. The gnome told him, in a ghoulishly bureaucratic tone, that the State had done its best and can devote no further special attention to his affairs. Berezov took it as an unsubtle but timely warning that winners don't do business with losers.

By the end of January Berezov managed to regain control of his affairs by shifting them away from locations known to the late and much-lamented Arumov.

Clearly, it would not be long before these locations were also discovered. But from now on Berezov only used former military installations that were superbly protected and unlikely to fall to an assault team with simple weapons, guarded as they were by armour with real firepower.

Similar protection was provided for Berezov's mansion, but just to be on the safe side he spent most nights in his headquarters in Moscow. He knew that authorities would have to react if someone mounted a full-scale assault – those days, as the gnome suggested, were coming to a rapid end. It seemed as though someone had decided to stake Russia's reputation on a civilized patina, constructed for foreigners in Moscow.

The general was virtually in hiding from his attackers. He saved face by putting about rumours that the "ghosts" attacked other organizations as well as his own. To give some truth to propaganda his men bombed drug warehouses and the odd discotheque belonging to competitors, without exerting themselves to minimize the loss of life.

Mironov's men slowly traced a few of the new locations and understood that the game had changed. None of targets could be forced by a commando assault, but that still left the convoys, going in and out of bases at random intervals.

The convoys were not a soft target either. Berezov's men packed cargo into heavy shipping containers hauled by prime movers hastily proofed against infantry weapons. Steel plates were welded over windows and engines, and chain skirts were hung from the sides to protect tyres from bullets.

Even anti-tank missiles were likely to be of dubious value. A large quantity of them may eventually stop such a vehicle but not break open the cargo, and an attempt to do so would probably be ended by machine gun emplacements on the roof of each truck, ably reinforced from with sizeable variety of escort vehicles whose arsenal included mortars mounted on beds of small trucks.

One target that incited particular temptation to brave these obstacles was a certain shipment. It left an old air force base in the south of the region just before dawn, moving at slow speed. This suggested enormous weight that was not evident from the state of the wheels. It was also notable that cargo-bearing vehicles travelled a considerable distance away from each other. The forward observer, immersed in the engine of a battered Moskvich as the convoy thundered past, concluded that it was carrying munitions.

Grishin's men discretely followed the convoy towards Moscow and overtook it at high speed on the highway leading north. Fifty kilometres ahead they turned around and stopped at the side of the road.

Before long the rest of the force raced past them towards the munitions convoy, Grishin's men tearing their clutches to fall in once they passed. They travelled for another ten kilometres, Mironov scanning the hurtling landscape for a good ambush location. He signalled an abrupt stop when they drove over a recently patched segment of road surface.

It spanned the full width of the concrete surface of the highway. A new drain had recently been laid beneath, the steel-reinforced bulk of the road bed being laboriously cut for this purpose. A pipe wide enough for a man to stand in was placed into the trench to link two sides of a boggy marsh, now concealed under snow.

Fresh concrete was poured over the top, but it was nowhere near as strong as the original surface, not to mention being undermined by the drain from beneath.

Mironov ordered the cars to keep going south and position themselves behind the convoy and out of its sight. The remainder of the force began to prepare an ambush.

Mironov listened to the report from the car shadowing the convoy and held out his hand with all fingers extended – four minutes at the most.

Six antitank missiles were placed into the drainpipe, pointing at various angles at the roof and secured by whatever could be found in the landscape. Mironov trained a telescopic sight on one of the warheads and took a few deep breaths to relieve tension.

When the convoy rumbled towards them he slid the safety catch and waited until the lead vehicle was within a few metres of the trap. He then fired, triggering a powerful detonation inside the drain.

The new concrete above the pipe was sent sky-high, leaving a deep gap in the road surface. The lead vehicle fell into it, being rammed by another from behind. The rest of the convoy managed to stop in time, but there was no question of reversing the semi trailers on a two-lane road surrounded by bog.

Missiles streaked from the trees, decimating the guards. Machine guns answered from the tops of the shipping containers, but they were blinded by the smoke and fired into the forest at random. Mironov ordered a missile into the gun emplacement of the lead truck. Unexpectedly, that triggered a massive detonation of the cargo, scattering the remains of the truck over a wide area. The defenders from other vehicles ran into the forest and were allowed to make their escape.

Mironov emerged onto the highway, rifle butt held against his shoulder. He lowered the barrel and waved an impatient gesture for the drivers of remaining trucks to leave their vehicles, and they scrambled down, holding their hands high in the air. One of Grishin's men searched them and waved them away. They scampered into the forest after the guards.

Car wrecks were pushed into the trench and driven over until they bridged the gap well enough to hold the weight of a truck. Then Mironov detailed three drivers to replace Berezov's men, who drove the hijacked convoy north at high speed.

Vehicles returned from the south to collect Mironov's contingent. The reconstituted convoy stopped at an intersection and swung into a country lane. They rattled past wheat fields towards a distant village, drove through its deserted street, followed the road over a hill into another forest and stopped to break open the containers. Mironov expected attack helicopters within one hour.

The payload was better than pure gold – boxes of ammunition and a few crates of new machine guns, still packed in factory grease.

"Take a look at these, Major," said Grishin, handing over a carton tube nearly two metres long.

Mironov studied the seal for a few seconds, then broke it and spread the contents on the truck tray. Grishin knelt to hold down the corners of a vast sheet of waxed paper covered in technical drawings.

They eventually divined that they were looking at a cutaway drawing of what appeared to be an attack helicopter with two giant rotors.

Mironov noted the "Top Secret" tag stencilled at the top right hand corner and hastily rolled up the plans.

"Put them some place safe," he told Grishin. He then jumped off the truck bed and stood next to it for a while, his forehead creased in deep thought.

***

The arms were sold to the burgeoning security market for a lot of money. That, Grishin assured, did not mean that they would end up in the hands of criminals. Not necessarily, especially if one was liberal and modern in defining crime.

Mironov was underwhelmed by that reassurance, but it looked very much as if his mission was nearing completion. It was time to think of his men, who selflessly spent two months not only risking their lives but also earning nothing, a reckless luxury for most citizens of new Russia.

A few more random hijackings were staged, but the payload was far less impressive – mostly bales of marijuana, which Mironov burned without unloading it from the vehicles. Later they found themselves in possession of a quantity of aviation fuel, which nearly met the same fate.

Grishin said that it would be diabolically difficult to sell – there was a lot of adulterated fuel around, and few people would take off in an aircraft tanked by someone they didn't know from past dealings. But Mironov didn't like the idea of setting fire to the tankers – even in winter such a fire would be immense, attracting much unwanted attention from authorities. They finally managed to offload the fuel to a shady dealer from Bulgaria, a vulgar man who clearly didn't care whether his customers' planes stayed in the air or not.

The latest hijacking produced a loot that was almost comical, and it said something about the effect they were having on Berezov's empire. The most he was now prepared to risk in transit were contents of a medium-sized supermarket. They were mainly dry goods, cleaning agents and low-value consumer items from a European nation that knew no lack of such products. One surmised that a shop in a small German town had gone bankrupt, and someone purchased its entire stock at a knockdown price, to be on-sold for many times that amount in Moscow, where the destitute were gradually edged out by bandit millionaires and their lackeys.

It was one of history's ironies that oil, once the focus of a hundred year struggle between Russian and British empires, was present on traditional Russian soil with abundance. All that was needed to liberate it was American technology, perfected on the fields of Alaska and Texas whose climatic extremes matched Russia's.

As any of Hitler's generals would attest, ordinary machinery does not work in the Russian cold, the grease hardening until it no longer lubricates, diesel fuel waxing up inside engines and steel becoming too brittle to carry its normal load.

Soviet heavy engineering was but a small advance on what was available to Hitler's armies and frequently much inferior. As a result, most oil deposits on the territory of the Soviet Union remained unexplored, their extraction awaiting equipment that reliably performed at climatic extremes and in difficult terrain.

In order to manufacture such equipment one requires a steel industry capable of pouring high-quality metal for ball bearings. Long-wearing ball bearings maintain the reliability of a manufacturing plant, allowing it to produce parts with little variation in size. The machines assembled from quality components in turn perform better and longer.

None of that was possible in USSR. Its engineers attempted to overcome quality problems by making parts larger and heavier, which made small variations in size less important.

That, in turn, exacerbated the Soviet thirst for fossil fuels, and the final result of that cascade was Mironov's presence in Afghanistan. That tragic country became a doormat, occupied in anticipation of a convenient time to join the neighbouring Iran to the fraternal union of socialist republics. As stated in a popular Russian joke, friendship of oppressed people knew no borders.

The broad strategy was nearly two centuries old, blocked by the British, who got to Iran first and occupied Afghanistan into the bargain. There was one attempt in 1920, but it proved too much for the fledgling Soviet regime. It tried again in 1941, but it was thwarted by Hitler's lightning strike at the heart of Soviet power. Instead, Stalin was forced into a humiliating negotiation with the Iranians, who begrudged some territory to be used as air bases during the war.

Mironov's first impulse was to leave the supermarket contents at the roadside and go, but then he was struck by another idea and asked for a map. Having made some calls, he ordered the convoy to a new destination, driving the lead truck himself.

Some hours of rough back roads later they reached a drab Soviet-era building surrounded by a tall cyclone fence. It stood on a low hill overlooking a small town with no distinguishing features.

Mironov drove up the hill at speed, splashing muddy snow from his tyres. He accelerated near the metal fence topped with razor wire, and his machine smashed through the gate without the slightest change in speed. Faded metal burst from tired hinges to be flung out of the way.

Mironov slowed down as he approached the grimy façade and stopped opposite a flight of steps that led to a gaol-like front door. He waited for other trucks to park and led his men into the building.

At the threshold their way was blocked by an

older man, a soiled baggy suit classic of Soviet bureaucracy hanging off his gaunt frame. Without a word Mironov threw out his arm, knife blade flashing in the grey light of a winter afternoon.

It slashed across the man's throat. It happened so fast that the target barely realized what had taken place, bringing up hands to the gash above his collar.

He slowly sank to the ground, looking at rivulets of blood that flowed down his torso. A loud wheeze was heard from the cut windpipe.

"Remember little Mironov?" asked his killer in a loud, searing whisper that seemed to border on reptilian hiss. "I hope so – because little Mironov will never be able to forget you."

The man's eyes opened with recognition for a moment, then glazed over and rolled behind puffy eyelids. Mironov stared at the dying man with an expression of smouldering fury, then brought up a boot and kicked him to the ground, stepping on the stilled face as he entered the building.

Everyone followed him into a dirty vestibule where an old man adorned in a dirty white apron frantically hobbled towards them on his wooden leg. He witnessed the entire scene but was coming towards Mironov with outstretched hands and a wide smile.

"Viktor," he shouted, his mouth showing a few remaining teeth. "Mother of God, it really is you."

"It is, Nikolai Alekseevich," Mironov threw down his bloodstained knife and embraced the old cook heartily, nearly lifting him off the floor. "I am sorry I took so long to return."

He jerked his thumb towards the corpse at the door. The cook hastily crossed himself.

"God works in mysterious ways," he pronounced coldly. "What goes around always comes around, but victims have to stay alive long enough to see justice done."

"Well, this victim stayed alive long enough," said Mironov. "After a fashion."

"Oh, you look pretty good to me," retorted Nikolai, standing back to size up Mironov with hearty approval. "Shoulders like a bear, not a gram of fat, and you move like a ghost – paratroops?"

"Better than that," replied Mironov proudly. "I made it into *spetznaz*."

"That'll be right," smiled Nikolai, extracting a packet of evil-smelling *Belomor* cigarettes. "I thought you will go far."

Mironov turned to his men.

"Welcome to my childhood home," he announced. "This is where they make men like me."

They nodded uncertainly.

"Take this thing away," he nodded at the corpse lying across the doorway. "Do me a favour, Vasily."

The man addressed snapped his heels and saluted. Mironov faced him and returned the salute.

"Drive it to the town square with a statue of Lenin – the one with its right arm outstretched towards bright future. String up a rope from that arm and hang this carrion by its feet. Attach a sign to say that all who prey on children can look forward to the same fate. Or worse, if we can spare a little time when we pass by next."

Vasily saluted again and set out to fulfil the order. Mironov turned to Nikolai, who was puffing on his nasty tobacco and nodding approval. The rest of the men began to unload the supermarket boxes and pile them inside.

"Our country seems fucked beyond recognition, my old friend," said Mironov vehemently. "I can't do anything about that, but I can still attend to the garbage in my own yard. That I can do."

"Don't fret, Viktor," replied Nikolai calmly.

"We've seen bad times before. We've lived through them, and we will live through this too. This is why we are Russians. Other nations can fight, and other nations can launch rockets, but no one else can endure what we are limping through now. And believe me, endure we will. Just by putting one foot in front of the other – that's our greatest military secret."

Mironov thought it over and smiled. He slapped the old man on the shoulder approvingly.

"It must be right if you say so," he replied. "Enough of this, old warrior – where the hell is everybody?"

"They are hiding," said Nikolai sadly. "Last time the children saw trucks like yours, many older ones were carted off, and we never heard from them again. There was some kind of talk about organ harvesting."

Mironov shook his head with force, the best interpretation of that gesture being a refusal to consider the implications of what he just heard.

"Go get everybody."

Nikolai hobbled off into a dark, stale-smelling corridor. Mironov picked up his knife, wiped the blade on a cardboard box and slit it open, removing a can of spaghetti labelled in German. He struggled with the writing and frowned, throwing the can back into the box.

Another box was more hopeful, yielding a trade quantity of cooking chocolate.

Nikolai came back with the remaining inmates of the orphanage – children of various ages, that spectrum ending abruptly just before puberty. They were dressed much as they would be in Mironov's day, in simple shapeless track suits, but one immediately apparent novelty was lack of sufficient nutrition and dental care. The wolf-cub stare in the eyes was about the same as ever, Mironov decided.

No other staff were in evidence, and he deduced that they had fled when they saw their boss being slaughtered. There were few clear consciences in a place like this, as he well knew.

Mironov began to toss chocolate blocks into the little crowd. Within seconds wary wolf-cubs turned into normal children, squealing with joy at the unexpected bounty.

"Don't eat these now," commanded Mironov as he threw out the last bar. "I want you to have something else first. Nikolai, kitchen detail, forward march!"

The officer's voice had the usual effect – all noise died down, children obediently stowed the chocolate, and kitchen detail emerged from the crowd to follow Nikolai to the kitchen. No one seemed to have even glanced at the pool of congealed blood at the door, which Mironov's men hastily moved to conceal with boxes. Another ran out to return with a pile of old burlap sacks from the truck. He tossed them down to soak what was left of the resident flesh merchant.

"What happens to them now?" asked one of his men sadly as he wiped his boot on a sack. "What is the plan for tomorrow?"

Mironov turned around.

"No plan at all," he replied. "You heard the old man – they just go on, putting one foot in front of the other. We didn't do anything that will change the world forever. Not every good deed has to."

Grishin smiled at his side.

"But Major," he said gently. "We did change something. No one will know how many lives you saved with a single stroke of your blade. The children who will not be abused, crippled or killed now have a shot at a normal human life, Major. A long shot, to be sure, but they might one day have children, and those will grow up like human beings. What you did will matter to their descendants forever, whether anyone else realizes or not."

Mironov nodded heavily, turning away to hide heavy tears sliding down his cheeks.

"And what great privilege that is for miserable butchers like you and me," continued Grishin, placing a hand on Mironov's shoulder.

Mironov swallowed hard and nodded without turning around.

"All we were destined to accomplish was demolition and murder," added Grishin, gripping Mironov's shoulder with strength. "Future generations were to remember us only by what we left – ruins, putrescence and hatred."

"But a single strike of your weapon returned hope to those destined for despair and suffering. I haven't seen much of that in my vile life, Major, so believe what I tell you – there is no greater honour for a man bearing arms."

Part III

Dressed in a heavy grey parka and felt boots, Minin stood at a plain bus stop on a plain February morning. The street was piled with dirty snowdrifts, and he was doing his best to avoid being splashed by wet snow from passing traffic.

Unlike public buses his transport came precisely on time. A brand-new Volkswagen van with tinted windows pulled up at the bus stop, ignoring angry horns from behind.

Its side door slid open, and Minin nimbly stepped inside, assisted by powerful arms which clamped onto both of his wrists. The gesture, however, was purely symbolic intimidation – they felt superior enough to not even bother with a body search.

The van rolled along the streets of Moscow, not lingering anywhere but not hurrying either. Minin shared the back of the van with four heavily bearded men with massive shoulders and dark eyes.

"Good day to you, Mustafa Ibrahimovich," he addressed their leader politely.

Mustafa Ibrahimovich Masaev, a man of indeterminate age but obvious fitness and virility, slowly shook his bold head, rifling stubby fingers through the greying beard.

"A good day it is not, Ivanushka," he replied, using a diminutive form of Minin's first name that is associated with a village idiot in Russian folklore. "I need that stuff in a hurry."

"I believe that my commander explained the circumstances."

"He tried," replied the Chechen gangster, shaking his head in disbelief. "But I am not sure I believe a single word. See, Ivanushka, I don't have much time for ghosts. There aren't any in the Holy Koran. Are there?"

He looked at each of his companions, who in turn shrugged shoulders with indifference.

"See – no ghosts," concluded Mustafa. "So what we have here is just nonsense, my friend. Just a plain Russian *bardak.*"

Minin did not react to that performance in any manner.

"To think your people once ran a huge empire," continued Mustafa, clearly enjoying the moment. "Look at you now – not even in control of your own streets."

"There are ups and downs in the history of every nation, as you know well," replied Minin acidly. "It is unwise to celebrate the demise of Russian power. To this humble observer, it is only just beginning to come into its own."

"Oh, yes," replied Mustafa severely. "We certainly felt your power in the Caucasus. Your troops proved very powerful against our women and children."

"That was a dirty conflict without possible winners, and you know what I think of that," replied Minin. "But let's not make grand statements. These are circumstances without precedent, and it is sometimes difficult for men regimented under the old system to react quickly. The general will succeed – he is a cunning, powerful fighter."

"Not as cunning as the man who hijacks his convoys, one thinks. And what now – you are asking our help! What are you offering?"

"You may keep the merchandise you capture," replied Minin. "We supply the intelligence and claim credit for the operations."

"That's outrageous!" exclaimed one of Mustafa's companions, a short man with enormous shoulders clad in a camouflage jacket.

"Not at all fair," agreed Minin. "But understand, that's the only way we can have it. It is absolutely unthinkable for us to allow the whole street to know how we ran out of muscle and had to resort to asking you for extra manpower. No, it's either your anonymous help or we crawl to the military, beg forgiveness and ask them to correct the situation. I am sure you can see how inconvenient that would be for all concerned."

"Your proposal is most amusing," replied Mustafa, his demeanour instead displaying a serious and thoughtful air. "I have to think it over."

"Not too long, please."

"Of course not," replied Mustafa irritably. "I am a mountain warrior, not one of your lowland ilk. Pull over."

The van stopped outside a nondescript building. Its deceptive blandness was ruined by three gleaming black Land Cruisers, parked in front of it in the snowdrifts. One of the men got out and walked from the van into the landing. A very short time later he returned, bearing a brass tray with a matching coffee pot and small cups in Arabic style.

Mustafa offered Minin one of the cups, and the Russian took it with a slight bow, accepting thick aromatic liquid personally poured by the gangster. It was an acknowledgement of their inevitable alliance.

Mustafa poured another cup for himself and passed the tray to his men. After waiting for them to fill their cups, the driver started the engine and drove down the street very gently. He seemingly aimed to prevent spillage of drink that cemented the brotherhood of former enemies, now united in ill intent.

He barely rounded the corner when a missile exploded just next to the van, throwing it on its side. Men poured from several neighbouring houses, fanning out to protect the van, but all were cut down by short bursts of automatic fire that seemed to come from all directions.

A few more missiles were fired into the row of Land Cruisers, enveloping the Chechen base in a curtain of flame that no human being could penetrate.

It was a superb outcome for an action organized at a moment's notice. Minin was tailed around Moscow, the strike force following a few blocks further back. When the target stopped for a few minutes, that short time was masterfully used to set up the assault team.

Mironov ran up to the cracked windscreen, machine pistol at the ready. The van's dazed driver managed to become upright and began to grapple with an assault rifle that was still trapped in twisted metal. Mironov fired a short burst into his head, turning the cabin into a sea of gore. He then circled the van casually, watching his men break open the rear doors to extract five occupants.

One of the Chechens tried to grasp a pistol at his

belt, but his arm was intercepted, twisted back and torn out of the shoulder socket. Others went quietly.

Facing Minin and Mustafa, Mironov safed his machine pistol and carefully replaced it in the holster. He stood ramrod-straight, his wide shoulders squared. One hand was slapping a leather glove against the other, the menace clear to his captives.

"Comrade Minin," he said with mock courtesy. "We meet at last. I hope I don't need to introduce myself."

"Major Mironov, of course," replied Minin, his voice shaking a little but expression remaining entirely neutral.

"That's right," said Mironov. "And this must be the great Mustafa. Well, I've heard of you. It takes a lot of courage to pimp and sell drugs on the streets of Moscow whilst your villagers are being slaughtered by Russian recruits and used like toilet paper by Arab criminals."

Mustafa turned pale but remained still. Mironov reached over and removed an Arab dagger with a jewelled handle from a scabbard at Mustafa's belt, examining the slightly curved blade that tapered to a pinpoint with approval.

"I actually don't have anything against your

kind," continued Mironov. "Your God, my God, any God – it's all the same to me. Isn't that curious – I've killed hundreds like you with my very hands, yet towards them I felt no anger. Just imagine what I will do to someone I hate. "

He studied both men as if they were specimens in a zoo.

"See, I have my little army and seem to be able to do whatever I please to superior forces," he resumed. "Do you know why that may be?"

"You tell me," replied Mustafa, his tone turning acrid. It was increasingly clear that he was not about to be killed.

"Because we are doing something worthwhile," Mironov told him. "We win because we cannot be out-manoeuvred. We cannot be outmanoeuvred because you cannot understand us. You cannot understand us because you only think about money and gratification of your animal desires. You are no longer capable of following the thought patterns of a man like myself. Or whatever I may be now."

"Fascinating," commented Minin, quite meaning it.

"Yes. So you see, I've come here to join your little meeting and ask Mustafa if he wants to become an obstacle in my path."

Mustafa stared at him and maintained silence, now in the throes of genuine indecision.

"I hope you realize what is happening," continued Mironov. "When it is finished, I shall grasp hold of Comrade Minin's boss and haul him down to the hottest part of hell, and no one on this earth is going to stop me. But living men can die trying, and I would like you to tell me if you want to be one of these corpses. That way I can make it happen now, without burning more fuel and without having more men killed."

He held up the dagger questioningly.

Mustafa shook his head resolutely.

"Wise decision," said Mironov. "Remember, my ancestors and yours did not always get along, but we are still here, both your kind and mine. You would want to think before you tamper with the formula of our co-existence."

Mustafa nodded curtly.

"Yes, very wise," Mironov rounded off his point. "So you have no need of him."

His right hand shot out to plunge the dagger into Minin's chest. Minin collapsed silently, a large blood stain spreading on his parka. His eyes were wide with surprise as he died.

"I also have a message for your mountain friends, Mustafa," continued Mironov quietly and purposely. "Warn them not to get carried away – it is not difficult to kill every one of you. We have that capability in Russia, and it would be very foolish to unleash it. That genie you will never stuff back into the bottle."

"My business is trade, not ideology," replied Mustafa. "I am not interested in politics."

"That would be very foolish if it were true," commented Mironov coldly. "I know Russia looks like a flea circus, but the bloodsucking insects in charge happen to command the world's largest nuclear arsenal and the world's most destructive army. Don't believe your own press about *Afgan* – it was not a defeat for us."

"How so?" asked Mustafa with a trace of smile.

"Very simply," answered Mironov wearily. "We did not come to that foul landscape to take it for ourselves. We weren't there to replace the native goat herders with Russian peasants. We went in to secure a few roads, and we did that in three months."

"You were losing a lot of men, and your government could not sustain it."

Mironov shook his head impatiently.

"At the height of our losses we were sending back just fifteen hundred coffins a year – in the Soviet days that was a small fraction of deaths from industrial accidents alone. By the time resistance appeared, our command had long fulfilled all of its required objectives. They were simply feeling lazy and comfortable, which is always a grave error. If they did their job they would have ordered us to kill every native alive, and we would have done that in another three months."

"But they hadn't and you didn't."

"That is so. An historic mistake, not to lock down that country and comb it from north to south, killing all civilians and starving the *Duhi* to death. But for that error, the Soviet Union would still be here, and if anyone wanted oil from any part of the Middle East, they would have had to ask nicely."

"That's very hypothetical."

"Of course. But take it as given that if I were charged with fulfilling such an order, there would be no Afghans left alive. I would turn the whole country into a mass grave without so much as having a bad dream. Do you doubt that?"

"No," replied Mustafa. "No, by Allah, that is the truth."

"Then it is wise to remember how many men like

me there are in Russia," Mironov told him with a note of sadness. "Do not push them to the top. That is how Russia reacts to a threat – we put a mass murderer on the throne."

He bent down to pull the dagger out of the dead man's chest, rinsed the blade in the snow and wiped the pink run-off on Minin's clothes. He handed the dagger back to Mustafa, handle first.

The Chechen took care to sheathe the weapon slowly and let his hand drop away from the belt. He squinted in thought as Mironov turned on his heel and left, flanked by his men.

***

Grishin drove yet another car procured from one of his contacts; both vehicles and addresses were now changed daily.

Mironov sat in the front passenger seat. His appearance was one of suddenly felt exhaustion.

Their progress was blocked by a traffic jam, unwelcome proof of new wealth now flowing into Moscow. Grishin braked with a curse, narrowly avoiding a slide into the truck he followed.

Mironov instantly came awake, his hands already working the slide of the machine pistol. He stopped as he assessed the situation and leaned back, rubbing his eyes with the backs of his gloved hands.

"Did you mean what you said to that *churka*?" asked Grishin, using a derogatory term for dark-haired natives of the Caucasus.

"Which part?"

"About God – you said you don't care."

"That's correct."

"But do you really think we are alone?" asked Grishin, staring at his commander. "Is that just a pleasant delusion, to hope there is a God?"

"No," replied Mironov, letting his hands fall

away from his eyes. "It is not a delusion."

Grishin noticed that the backs of Mironov's gloves were dark with moisture. He swivelled in his seat, waiting for his commander's next words with intense concentration. Mironov sensed it and opened his blood-shot eyes, shaking his head.

"God exists," he continued quietly. "It is us. We are God. Everything our ancestors had done. What we do now. Everything is God, and that everything, in turn, dictates our actions. To a certain point."

"You surely don't mean that we are in charge," replied Grishin, his posture loosening slightly.

"No, I don't mean that Marxist-dialectic drivel. Individually we are not in control of anything. Our reality is a collective product of our minds and actions, from the beginning to the end. What we do, what we say and to what we aspire – that is what the ancients called God, and nothing has changed."

"Do you say this because of what happened to you?"

"Yes," answered Mironov. "Possibly. But I don't want to analyze it – there is simply no purpose in that."

"So is that it? Do we worship ourselves?"

"Why not? It is better than what we were trained to believe, my old friend," replied Mironov, leaning back into the seat. "If we all accepted that life is sacred, that all repository of thought is precious – why, in such a world you and I would have to find honest work."

The traffic jam cleared slowly. Grishin restarted the engine and crawled along the street, thinking.

"God is us," he repeated quietly, trying the words on his tongue. "All of us? Like Berezov? How about our marinated President?"

"Perhaps not all humans belong with God," replied Mironov sleepily. "Who knows? Maybe you and I are not a sick aberration after all. Perhaps there is a reason for having executioners in creation."

***

They stopped at a nondescript house where Grishin nodded to three men emerging from the landing. Mironov grasped Grishin's shoulder in a farewell gesture and followed them inside.

They rode a lift to one of the apartments provided by Grishin. Mironov constantly moved between these dwellings, apparently vacated at short notice by their occupants.

He came into the vestibule with three men, who made themselves comfortable near the door. Mironov removed his coat and took off the body harness with his machine pistol.

Another man was waiting for him to undress before approaching and saluting. His gesture was crisply returned, then Mironov nodded for him to speak.

"We completed target reconnaissance, Major," said the man, proffering Mironov a topographic map with profuse pencil markings. "This is the location of the mansion, and these marks indicate sentry positions."

"Anything heavy?"

"Yes, Major. Machine gun coverage of the entire sector, a few rockets and one light anti-aircraft gun. Berezov seems to be scared – he hasn't been out in two weeks."

Mironov studied the map closely.

"That's about a hundred men, Captain" he replied with a dark frown. "It's going to be an abattoir."

"Yes, sir."

"So be it," continued Mironov after some hesitation, his jaws tightening with resolve. "No shortage of room in hell. Call the squad leaders – we will plan something for later. Two weeks isn't long enough – we will make them sweat for a month, then strike just as they begin to tire from constant alert."

He returned the map and nodded his thanks. The scout saluted and left the flat.

Mironov heard Nina's voice and went into the kitchen.

Nina held the phone with shaking hands, tears streaming down her swollen face. She listened and nodded occasionally, sobbing.

Whatever it was that she spoke about, every sentence from the other end increased her distress. Mironov stood next to her, half-expecting to be told to leave. She glanced in his direction but continued to listen without a further reaction to his presence.

Then she put down the phone and covered her

face in a gesture of utter despair.

Mironov sat next to her and touched her shoulder awkwardly. At length she looked up, her eyes remaining unfocussed.

"What is it?" asked Mironov for the hundredth time. She thought briefly and seemed to come to a decision.

"Come with me," she stood up abruptly. "Alone."

He waited for her at the door. When she appeared from the bedroom he took the machine pistol off the hook.

"That won't be necessary," she said shortly.

He replaced the gun on the hook, instead accepting a small pistol from one of his men. He slipped it into a pocket of his leather coat and opened the door for Nina, gesturing to his men not to follow.

They took one of the Jeeps, and he followed her directions to a drab Soviet-era building of red brick, in which she pointed out an entrance. She took his arm and lead him into a evil-smelling stairwell, where they climbed to the third floor.

"Here's my story," she said, her voice hard and hoarse with pain. "My son is in this hospital. Has been, for the past six months. "

"What's wrong with him?" asked Mironov.

"Leukaemia," she replied. "That's why I whored. They can't afford the right treatment. You have to buy it yourself."

"Where is his father?" asked Mironov bitterly.

"Somewhere in the Kamchatka, in his helicopter," replied Nina. "Flew into a mountain six years ago. They never found him."

"What's going on now?" Mironov stopped as he opened the door to the ward. Nina stared at him, eyes wide with despair.

"It's over," she whispered, fresh tears springing onto her cheeks. "They just told me he has pneumonia. He has relapsed, and they can't stop it any more. There is nothing else left to try."

Mironov shook his head in horror. He took Nina by the hand, and they walked through the cancer ward, assailed by smells of stale vomit and pain. She grasped his hand with inhuman strength and walked on.

They came to the last room in the corridor, past the nurses who saw them and looked away. Nina opened the door and walked into semi-darkness.

Mironov let go of her hand and reeled at the sight. A small body lay in a large hospital bed, topped by a head with no hair, a smooth yellow dome that sank into white sheets. There was no smell and no sound – just a dim light that shone on the yellow face from the broad window.

"Mama," whispered the child. His tiny hand, all yellow skin stretched over bone, made its way from beneath the blankets, touched Nina's fingers and rested on her hand.

"Mama is here," said Nina, her voice surprisingly strong. "Mama is with you now."

"That's good," replied the boy with a faint smile. "They say I am dying, Mama. Is that right?"

"I don't know," said Nina, suddenly breathless with pain. "I don't..."

She began to sob uncontrollably.

"It doesn't hurt," said the little boy gently.

Nina nodded, her eyes streaming. Mironov came to stand behind her and put both hands on her shoulders, grasping hard. She leaned against him, shuddering slightly.

"Mama, it feels like I am going some place. Can you tell me where?" asked the boy.

"I..." Nina stuttered. "I don't know that either..." She covered her face and stayed still, then looked up into her son's eyes. He stared back earnestly.

Mironov suddenly shivered with chill. The hospital room faded, and he was inside his tank, acrid smoke filling the hull. He felt the metal of the pistol in his hand, and sweat stung the cuts on his forehead.

"Where am I going?" he thought in sudden panic.

The vision faded, and he found himself back in the hospital room, clutching Nina's shoulders for support against increasing vertigo.

"Goodbye, Mama," he heard a whisper. "I am going to sleep now. I don't think I will wake up again."

She flung herself at the bed and held her son with all desperation. Mironov saw a tiny yellow hand tenderly fold around her neck.

Nina stayed still as the hand slid down and came to a gentle rest on the blanket.

It was a long time before she moved, and when she did, it was with infinite care, as if not to wake the young child she finally let go. She unwound her arms and straightened slowly. Mironov saw that the boy had ceased breathing, his yellow-tinged blue eyes wide-open and still.

Nina uttered a moan of visceral pain and buried her face in the blankets. Mironov stood next to her, one hand on her convulsing shoulders. He reached over and, with a practised slide of the other hand, closed the boy's eyes.

As he touched the papery skin the vertigo became worse and overcame his balance. A very fit man, he found this a new sensation for very soon he could no longer stand, staggering towards the nearest wall to slide down to the floor.

He became aware of being numb as his vision faded in twilight. There was a sensation of being rapidly propelled through empty space, and he was racked with nausea and panic. It lasted a very long time, then the numbness slowly receded, and he was again able to see.

The hospital room was now in darkness, and he realized that he was slumped against the wall on the floor. He made out Nina, who motionlessly knelt by the bed, her head resting next to her son's. At first Mironov was unable to move, but sensation and control gradually returned to his limbs.

Some hours later Nina stood up, covered her son's face with the blanket and turned with finality. Mironov took her hand, and they left the room, walking down the hospital corridor slowly. They went down the stairs and reached the Jeep, where Mironov opened the door for Nina.

She leaned onto his shoulder and held him hard for a few moments. Mironov put his arms around her and stood still, sharing her distress and feeling how he cushioned that impact.

After a few precious minutes Nina broke the embrace and climbed into the Jeep. He shut the door and stared at her for a moment, then marched around and started the engine.

"Home," he said grimly. Nina nodded.

They drove to her apartment, parking the Jeep in a little street around the corner from the building. They came through the armoured door into the landing, Mironov's hand on the pistol inside the coat. But no one challenged them – Berezov's men had obviously left.

They took the lift and entered, her apartment still bearing the marks of invasion. Nina picked up an upturned chair from the floor and sat down, lowering her head onto her arms.

Mironov found vodka and made her drink a large portion. He then took the glass away but realized that he too craved the spirit and drank a mouthful straight from the bottle.

It went down like fire, but he swallowed hard and drank some more. He threw down the empty bottle and led Nina into her bedroom, where they gently drifted off to sleep on top of an unmade bed.

Mironov awoke in pre-dawn darkness, Nina breathing into his shoulder quietly. He disengaged from her gently and left the flat, marching back to the car. He climbed in and pulled out the phone.

"Where the hell were you, Major?" asked Grishin, his voice betraying agitation.

"You don't want to know," replied Mironov. "But I will be over soon."

***

A few hours later he faced a line of the men who looked at him expectantly.

"The final stage of the operation is cancelled," was all he said.

There were angry murmurs as they processed the implications of his order.

"The place is packed with ordinary men," explained Mironov, putting up his hand in a call for silence. "Over a hundred guards, former soldiers, our comrades. Their only crime is that they need Berezov's dollars to feed their families. They have their orders, and if we move on the general, those men will die. Not to mention many of us, as well."

"We captured enough money to compensate everyone," he continued. "No one will be out of pocket."

"So you will just let the fucker off?" asked a grizzled veteran, who stood next to Mironov clutching a sniper rifle.

"Absolutely not," replied Mironov. "He will be dealt with, but not through a private war waged on the streets amongst innocent people. There is another way."

He saw their eyes and knew what they would not say. They decided that he had sold out.

"You will see what I came up with very soon," said Mironov forcefully. "But there will be no more violence and no further bloodshed. All my life I had killed and burned, I poisoned and destroyed, and this is where it stops."

He looked around and locked eyes with every man briefly. There was complete silence.

"I, Guards Major Viktor Maratovich Mironov, order the meat grinder to halt!" he shouted at the top of his voice.

Grishin was the first to react. He drew himself to rigid attention and snapped his arm in salute.

"Yes, Comrade Major," he replied quietly and distinctly.

With that, it was over. Weapons were lowered, the wolf stares lost focus, and crouched postures eased. Then the line broke up as men turned on their heels and went away.

Mironov returned Grishin's salute, and the two men embraced, tears rolling down their cheeks.

***

Three hours later a train pulled into an isolated station a little out of Moscow. It passed a few desultory dachas clad in deep snow, slowing to stop at a short platform whose station house was locked in view of the long day drawing to an end.

Not that the station of that remote forest settlement lost much business. Few wished to share its isolation on a late winter afternoon, and the beauty of snow-clad surroundings looked a little wan in sinister silence.

A few straggling skiers, who had spent an enviable day on forest trails, boarded the sooty carriages. After a few minutes the whistle blew a note, and the locomotive lurched forward, belched blue smoke and slowly gathered speed. Another minute later the train rounded the bend and disappeared into the forest.

The sole reminder of its passing was an elderly FSB officer with colonel's insignia, who was left standing on the platform. He was clad in a heavy winter greatcoat, pistol at his belt. The colonel ran his eyes over the distant tree line and turned away, signalling contempt for whatever danger awaited within.

Mironov emerged from the forest already combed for ambush by his men. He made his way towards the station on skis, a cylindrical container strapped across his back like a long-barrelled rifle.

At Mironov's approach the colonel turned around, and his haughty expression melted to joy at what he saw.

"Vitya!" he exclaimed with exuberance. "So it is true."

Mironov stopped just short and planted his poles in the snow. He straightened rigidly and saluted. The salute was returned, then the colonel grabbed Mironov's hand and gripped it with all his strength.

"I don't know what, if anything, is true, Comrade Colonel," replied Mironov. "I hope you may know something I don't."

"About your... reappearance? Nothing, I am sorry to say. I pulled out the army file and had a look – all seems bullet-proof to me. An explosion that shredded your tank to splinters. No remains and a symbolic funeral. I swear that's all there is in the documents."

Mironov became stock-still and stared past the colonel into the forest, absorbing that information. He trusted his old instructor absolutely, and if the old master who once trained him in infiltration techniques said so, the last hope of making sense of Mironov's existence suddenly evaporated, a misty breath exhaled into a winter afternoon.

For once in his life Grishin was wrong. An event

that defied rational explanation still remained a mystery after perusal of official documents. That rare occasion offended the Russian mindset, which instantly attributes all inexplicable events to government machinations – usually with great accuracy.

"Thank you," replied Mironov at some length.

"Again, Vitya, I am sorry."

"Yes," Mironov's voice again turned brisk and hard. "But that was not why I called you."

He removed the cylindrical container from his back and handed it to the colonel.

"I would stake my life on your honesty and do so now," he said, staring into the colonel's heavy-lidded blue eyes. "I need this to reach the right people. The contents speak for themselves, I attached a statement to outline how they came into my possession."

"Easily done," replied the colonel, removing a mobile phone from his pocket. "Provided this satanic thing works, I am going to place your package on the right desk by morning."

He selected a number and dictated his location, then cut the call.

"Done," he concluded with a short, sad smile. "Vitya, are you all right? Anything I can do?"

"I don't yet know the answer to either," replied Mironov, his voice turning brittle.

"I understand. Or, more truthfully, I don't. But you know where to find me when you need me."

"Thank you, Comrade Colonel."

"There is more, Vitya. Listen, we are not as specialized as we used to be, if you know what I mean. We all get wind of what goes on, and I've heard a few things you need to take into account."

"Always."

"That ghost army of yours... It is about to be disbanded, Vitya. I suggest you do that yourself before our head breakers do it on someone's order."

"I understand, Comrade Colonel."

"Yes. Apparently, we are not interested in getting involved, but you know the sensitivities. Our great entrepreneurs are behind the new rulers. Their voices ring loud in the halls of the Kremlin, and they largely get their way. Those whose business it is are working on a more suitable solution, but it will not be implemented in a hurry. We've had enough of dizzy reform."

"What is happening is intolerable."

"Of course. But there are sensibilities to be observed, Vitya, otherwise we will end up with the same brothel as our present leadership. So you see, blatant *spetznaz* assaults on our oligarchs are very inconvenient. Especially as masterfully planned and executed as they have been. Mother of God, someone might conclude that I am behind these operations."

"I will be honoured if they do, Comrade Colonel."

"As will I. But this business, arming resentful veterans... Ordinary bandits we nurture, Vitya. But messages of resentment delivered with rocket-propelled grenades – heavens, we cannot let that become a pattern. If only you robbed that vermin for the money."

"Valuable information indeed."

"I need say no more. Now leave me, Vitya. I have no idea who is coming for me."

They again exchanged salutes and shook hands.

"Oh, one thing, Vitya," called out the colonel as Mironov began to turn on his skis.

"Yes, Comrade Colonel."

"When you finish with the loose ends, put your head down and disappear yourself," said the older man forcefully. "No patriotic gestures and no politics. Hang up your uniform and get a quiet job in the security industry some place. Otherwise you are going to be a corpse before spring."

"I will do my best," said Viktor pensively. "It is hard to ignore what is happening."

"Vitya, Vitya," the colonel shook his head in disapproval. "You surely know history better than that. To make a difference you have to be at the top. The actions of ordinary people don't matter in the slightest – and that will never change in Russia. You are never going to be *nomenklatura* – that requires a mindset which you, I am pleased to say, do not possess."

Mironov nodded in sad acquiescence and completed his turn. He gathered speed and disappeared into the forest using a skating stride he had just learned.

It had revolutionized his favourite sport, placing the confounded Americans ahead of the Russians in all the championships where non-Russian names were once rare at medal presentation. Mironov decided to learn it for that reason alone, finding a pair of newfangled skating skis and practising the use of their feather weight and razor-sharp edge that made them mimic skates on firm snow.

In truth, it was a miserable, frog-like action, not at all like the graceful diagonal stride that is the joy of every Northern European. But there was no denying that the frog stride bore him into the forest with once unimaginable speed.

There was a tiny movement in the undergrowth at three other locations around the station. Mironov's snipers abandoned their observation posts and raced through the forest to regroup around him.

Nothing was being left to chance in what Mironov now considered a very dangerous game. He did not feel the slightest concern after attacking a criminal gang, but playing chess with the government was a totally different proposition. The fact that the latest reincarnation of Russian autocracy chose to let criminals control the streets did not make that government any less sinister – contemptible certainly, but also unpredictable.

The old colonel's warning contained nothing of surprise. Rather than briefed, Mironov was handed a valuable offer of a face-saving exit. Mironov understood this entirely, and his reaction, down to the last flicker of the eyelids, was crafted to signal that the offer was accepted. Now, instead of troubling themselves to exterminate his men, the authorities knew to do no more than deny their existence.

Mironov had no compunction about involving his

men in a campaign against Berezov, but he now felt a grave responsibility to sweep away the tracks of its participants.

The stakes were high. Security services noticed an armed group whose purpose was not banditry, and that scrutiny would not take long to translate into ill health.

***

The funeral was as short as the life it farewelled. There was only a handful of mourners, all family who greeted Mironov cautiously through muffled tears. They looked as if they had long given up any hope of the child surviving and were simply relieved that Nina's nightmare was finally over.

Snowflakes drifted across a still-sunny sky in premonition of a winter storm. The air became unseasonably warm and still.

A junior priest quietly intoned his prayers, evidently embarrassed by his youth. Nina sobbed quietly and clutching Mironov's hand. It was only when she kissed the proffered cross of simple chrome and dropped a handful of earth on the plain wooden coffin that she broke down, burying her head in the coarse wool of his greatcoat. He wore dress uniform, and he was reasonably certain that he wore it for the last time.

Afterwards the priest briefly held her hand and spoke of afterlife. Mironov listened on Nina's behalf and released the priest with a thankful nod. For a while the family huddled around the grave that gaped amid frozen ground, then drifted away.

Nina remained still, her gaze riveted to the mound of churned soil. When shadows of denuded trees began to lengthen, Mironov took her hand and gently led her away from a shiny metal cross rammed into earth, but the afterglow from it haunted their vision until they turned a corner.

They had a long way to walk, trudging through fresh snow which obscured the cemetery pathways. Nina took his hand, and they slowly walked past the traffic that pushed its way through February slush.

***

A convoy of BTR's rumbled through the fresh snow on Kutuzovskoe *Shossé*, the highway leading out of Moscow towards pristine forests. It was home to many exclusive *dacha* precincts.

The armoured vehicles slowed down the traffic for many kilometres, averaging just sixty kilometres an hour on the reinforced concrete surface. They turned off the highway an hour from the city and rattled down a country lane, spraying freshly fallen snow from their tracks.

The convoy stopped a little distance into the forest because of a tractor-like vehicle parked across the road. Berezov's men came out of the cabin, one of them making a forceful gesture to halt.

He was shown to the back of the lead vehicle. An officer with the insignia of a captain of interior troops nimbly jumped from the rear hatch.

"FSB business," he spat. "Radio all your thugs and tell them to desert their posts."

Berezov's guard looked at him dumbly.

"Read this order, worm bait," commanded the captain, splaying open his map case. "Then fucking well do what I say."

The guard peered at the close typeface on a piece of paper, which was lodged in a clear plastic protector.

"Holy Mother," he whispered. "The President..."

"That's right," replied the officer. "Radio now. I have no wish to kill anybody."

The guard hurriedly extracted a hand-held radio and spoke into it furiously. He then threw the radio into the snow and looked at the officer expectantly.

"Now get out of our way," barked the latter, gesturing to the vehicle blocking the road with impatience. He turned and climbed inside the *BTR*, doors swinging shut behind him.

The guard ran back to his vehicle and frantically gunned the engine, billowing black smoke as he drove off the road into young firs. The convoy charged past, emerging from the forest into an open field that surrounded Berezov's mansion.

Without warning the vehicles turned and splayed out in fan formation, surrounding the hill that stood in the middle of a wide expanse of wheat stubble poking through snow.

The lead vehicle continued down the road. Its driver saw a black Mercedes bolt towards them, but its escape was a fraction too late. The driver fishtailed to a stop and reversed into the yard, wrought-iron gates sliding shut behind him.

The *BTR* stopped a length short of the solid fence that suddenly looked as flimsy as paper. The carrier's automatic cannon left its resting position and rose ten degrees, pointing forward with menace.

"General Berezov," thundered the loudspeaker. "You are surrounded by forces of the Federal Security Bureau. You will come out of the house with your hands in the air and come with us."

There was no reaction from the house.

"Take down the gate," ordered the captain, studying the scene through the driver's hatch.

A short volley was fired point-blank into the pillar supporting the gate. It exploded in a shower of masonry that sprayed the house with hurtling brick fragments, smashing a few windows. The gate hinges hung loose for a few seconds, then the ironwork crashed to the ground.

A few moments after the dust settled the front door was cracked open, and a male hand holding a white sheet was waved in plain view.

"Come out slowly," ordered the captain into the megaphone. "Do not attempt any resistance. My orders are to kill anyone who resists, including yourself."

The door opened a little more, and General

Berezov stepped out into fading sunshine. He stood at the entrance, ramrod-straight in a dark grey suit with a faint white stripe. His hands were held at shoulder height perfunctorily, and the mouth was slightly creased in a smile – part contempt, part irony.

He slowly walked out into the centre of the circular driveway and stopped.

"What is the meaning of this circus?" he asked in a loud, even voice.

"General Berezov," replied the captain into the megaphone. "You are under arrest for disclosure of state secrets."

Berezov's eyebrows flickered in a small display of discomfiture, then his face creased in genuine amusement as he approached the *BTR* and stood beside it.

"What kind of secrets?" he demanded with a smile, lowering his hands. "What kind of state?"

"Mine is a simple job," replied the officer, lowering the megaphone. "Officially, I've been ordered to take you in, dead or alive. Unofficially, I was told to find a reason to open fire. However you are a fellow decorated veteran, and you will not be mistreated by anyone under my command. Provided you reciprocate my respect."

"But these are farcical charges, young man," said Berezov evenly.

"You can discuss this at headquarters," replied the captain coldly. "Everything will be clarified there."

Berezov's eyes hardened on hearing a phrase that has chilled Russians for three generations. Unlikely to lose its relevance any time soon, it implies that the individual addressed is already sentenced, and all that remains is to read the verdict and dispose of the prisoner as dictated by powers unseen.

But Berezov was not ordinary fodder. He owned his era and, like many before him, considered himself fireproof.

"You are to come around to the rear hatch and board," ordered the captain through the megaphone. "The remainder of your household is to remain inside until we leave."

The general nodded to these instructions. He circled the *BTR*, staring ahead woodenly. Rear doors swung open to reveal two troopers who trained their assault rifles on his chest. Berezov shook his head at the redundancy of it.

The truth was that even in the anarchy of that time a letter sent to his address would probably have achieved the same result as sending an entire armoured column. Berezov knew, as only a high-ranking servant of his state could know, that resistance against the will of Russian government is a gesture of utter madness. The hope lay in being close to some people in that government.

"Let me see the order," he demanded crisply. The officer splayed open his map case, and Berezov read it calmly, suppressing a flicker when he read the name at the bottom.

An attempt to escape would be marginally more rational, but he would have to run very far to be safe. Given his age and lack of familiarity with the outside world, many others would need to be involved in that escape. The resultant camouflage was very vulnerable to bribery and blackmail, and the state he once served needed no tuition in the use of those tools.

He boarded the *BTR* and sat down on the ice-cold bench, soldiers swinging the doors shut behind him. Engines roared, and the convoy sped away, the machines encircling the house reversing to fall into formation on the road.

Once back on the highway, the convoy ran towards Moscow at top speed, breaking up fresh snow to the delight of motorists. They were at the city limits within an hour, rumbling down the wide avenue's centre lane, reserved for official traffic from the days of Stalin.

As they sped towards their destination, two pedestrians studied the convoy from the sidewalk, standing amid piles of dirty snow that turned blue in fading light.

"Is that it?" asked Nina.

Mironov nodded grimly, staring at the armour until it turned a corner and disappeared out of sight.

The vehicles drove on until they came to a wide square, once dominated by a huge statue of a diminutive Polish Jew. He founded what later became Cheka, NKVD, MGB, more famously the KGB and currently known as FSB.

As it traversed acronyms, that institution killed more Jews than the Third Reich, but that does not prevent Russians from accusing Jews of fomenting the October Revolution to feather their nests.

That statue once set off a stolid commercial building that pre-dated the revolution. Its original industrious purpose was altered, making its stately façade one of the most hated on the planet.

Name changes bore even less resemblance to function. The statue has been torn down, but cellars beneath the building remain just as dark, the blood stains on the walls of interrogation rooms just as fresh. Control exerted by the occupants of this building over the largest country on earth is as complete as ever. If nothing else, that control is now more masterful than ever, concealed as it is behind a veneer of democracy.

Another set of gates slid open, and the retired general crossed them with little trace of his arrogance, handcuffed to a cold metal bench.

The lead *BTR* clattered into the centre of a large courtyard where countless men have disembarked from the last ride of their lives. The engine stopped.

After the gates were shut, the general's handcuffs were removed, and he was led outside. He was met by a squad of guards who applied their own handcuffs rudely and tightly, then marched him off as their sergeant signed the prisoner transfer.

He was led inside the building and down a long corridor with baize carpets and surprisingly good wooden panelling. It led to a set of lifts, where the squad left him alone with two guards. They summoned a lift and ordered him inside.

He watched a guard select a button for one of the underground levels, applying a key to the switch panel.

"Where am I being taken?" he asked in a commanding voice.

Neither guard acknowledged the sound of his

voice, the lift creeping down. Floors went by slowly.

"Answer me, damn it," he ordered the nearest man.

The guard slammed his elbow into Berezov's midriff without moving a single facial muscle. The general doubled over on the filthy floor of the lift and gasped for breath.

The lift came to a halt, and the guards lifted him off the floor without a trace of aggression, leading him down the dimly lit corridor. He became dizzy thinking he was being put into a cell, but that was not to be.

The door at the end of the corridor led to a large interrogation room, whose walls appeared to be green in the semi-darkness. There was no furniture apart from a very heavy armchair, set in concrete in the middle of the room. Soiled leather restraints hung from both of its chrome arms.

He was pushed into it, and his handcuffs were removed. He was then left alone in the room.

After nearly an hour the door swung open again, and he was confronted by a stout older man with colonel's insignia. His uniform was FSB, but the bearing was old-school military, seldom found in the ranks of interior troops.

Berezov realised how much it disconcerted him not to see the man's eyes in dim light. The colonel stopped a metre away and stood still, glaring at his quarry.

"Oh, general," he said suddenly, his voice full of pity.

It was all he needed to do to unleash a torrent of babble – they had the wrong man, the charges were ludicrous, he could surely explain and hopes to clear up any misunderstanding...

The colonel listened to the first few minutes impassively, then shook his head.

"General," he said, shaking his head slowly. "There is no mistake."

Berezov fell silent, staring at the man with horror.

"We have you cold, General," he was told. "One of your convoys was hijacked by bandits a few months ago. Now, one of them turned out to be a true patriot, and a weapons expert to boot."

Berezov gasped, making instant sense of that statement.

"The bandits found a report on the new helicopter," continued the colonel. "The one that shows its vulnerable points. That document was headed to the Caucasus, was it not?"

Berezov stared at him silently.

The colonel grabbed his lapels, lifting the prisoner out of the metal chair to throw him back with force.

"Answer me, traitor!" he shouted with anger that had Berezov cringe, but he maintained silence.

"What was it?" asked the colonel. "Guns for drugs? That's what Muslim guerrillas do normally, don't they? That's how you traded with them all your life, did you not?"

Berezov maintained his stare without a visible reaction.

The colonel slammed a gloved fist into his mouth. Berezov hit the chair with the back of his head, seeing stars. The dimly lit room swam before his eyes as he felt the restraints tighten around his wrists, binding him fast in the chair.

He felt the colonel's breath on his left cheek.

"This will go on, General," he hissed in fury. "I have a son at the Chechen front. He didn't want to spend his days pulling out fingernails like his father, so he is now an infantry captain, and he flies in those helicopters all the time. So we will be here until you talk or we will be here for the rest of your life, whichever may be the shortest."

What followed felt like a blur to Berezov. He was beaten, doused in cold water, electrocuted with a pair of wires the colonel pulled from a niche on the wall, choked until he passed out and had his testicles slowly squeezed by a merciless steel grip that made him vomit.

Some hours later Berezov dictated a confession, barely moving his pulped lips. It took a while to write down everything he knew about the Chechen criminal gangs that operated in Russia and sent proceeds of their trade to the guerillas. His arms were then released from restraints, and he was given a drink of water.

The colonel went away with the statement. By Berezov's reckoning he returned less that an hour later, staring at him sadly.

"Well, General," he said at last.

Berezov looked at him, head swimming from the pain. He understood that something crucial was about to happen.

"I am sorry, but you know yourself, General," continued his tormentor. "The sentence for what you have done is death. None of your filthy drug dollars can change that."

"We will see what happens in court."

Without a sound the colonel produced an envelope from the inside pocket of his tunic. He extracted a sheet of thick grey paper, and Berezov's exhausted gaze sharpened as he studied the crest and the seal across a broad signature.

He made out a verdict of a military tribunal. As an officer of the reserve, he was subject to its rulings.

He had been stripped of rank, decorations and all privileges awarded for service in combat. In addition, Berezov was to be executed at the site of incarceration, forthwith. A shameful death meted out to murderers and rapists once their appeals, inevitable and inevitably fruitless, were dispensed with.

That procedure called for an executioner to march the condemned man down a dark basement corridor, ordering him not to turn around. Without warning, a low-calibre pistol would be fired into the back of the head point-blank, preventing significant spillage of brain, bone and even blood.

Prisoners with mental defects would spend an entire shift cleaning the corridor entirely, preventing the next condemned man from panicking at the site of execution.

That apparently humanitarian gesture was, in fact, calculated to minimize the number of those who participated in executions. Few prisoners expected their death when it came, requiring no restraints as they trod their last path. Even the Soviet state recognized that such duties forged undesirable character traits and kept down the numbers of those involved.

That grisly pantomime was a world away from the death of a gallant officer at the hand of a gallant enemy, that final dignity of high rank. There would be no macabre romance of smoking the last cigarette, studying the firing squad with bone-chilling contempt, straightening his uniform and bellowing the order to fire.

"Alert the President before you even think of carrying out that sentence," whispered Berezov hoarsely. "Otherwise expect another such document by dawn, bearing your name."

Remaining silent the colonel produced another envelope with an expression that looked like regret. Berezov did not need to see the contents, but they were displayed for him regardless. In a single line of text the ruler of all Russia affirmed that he was aware of the court martial and endorsed its decision.

"This incident gives me no pleasure," the colonel carefully restored both documents to their respective envelopes. "In fact, I feel nauseous –

fellow veteran and all that. So what say we short-circuit the usual proceedings?"

He opened his hand, revealing a small white capsule. He put it between thumb and finger and slowly rolled it before Berezov's eyes.

The general nodded slowly.

His interrogator slipped the capsule into the breast pocket of Berezov's shirt and left. He shut the doors behind him respectfully.

Berezov reached for the pill with a trembling hand, and his bruised fingers closed around the gelatine globule. He grasped firmly and removed it from the pocket, studying the tiny white object with horror.

He thought for a long time, weighing up a myriad different facts and figures. After a few minutes his brain refused further overload.

Berezov slowly brought his hand to the battered lips and dropped the capsule onto his tongue, swallowing it with a small amount of blood that was trickling in his mouth.

He soon passed out.

One drug kept him mercifully unconscious. The second took longer to dissolve in the acid of his stomach, then flooded his blood stream with cyanide.

A second later Berezov gasped for air despite deep sedation, then his head lolled onto his chest. He died, a trickle of bloody saliva running down the stained silk of his shirt.

***

Epilogue

They went all the way home on foot, and it took many hours. Mironov and Nina walked the streets of Moscow hand in hand, the day fading around them slowly.

Snowflakes swirled and landed on their bare heads, cars sloshed past and pedestrians flowed around them. They did not hurry despite having to traverse a considerable distance. For both it was a journey long overdue, and there was no rush to see it out.

They made steady progress, snow creaking under their feet. The air was warm, indicating an imminent blizzard, and Mironov's mind kept returning to a small grave that would vanish under snow by the morning. At that thought something felt as if it tore inside his chest, a new sensation he found humbling and painful.

Nina maintained the peaceful calm of one who simply feels no need to speak. Russians consider it rude to remain silent in the company of strangers, and her silence said that she accepted Mironov in full.

He too maintained silence, but his mind still whirled, as it always did at the completion of something he expected to backfire.

Grishin and his fellow sergeants made themselves unavailable with little persuasion. One negotiated a long holiday in Spain for his family, and the second decided to emigrate to his daughter's town in New Jersey.

Grishin himself divined that winter is an excellent time to visit the Holy Land. He had a lot of grievances to present to God, and he proposed to do so by praying at every stop along the traditional pilgrim trail.

In addition, he was planning to escort old Natalya Fedorovna to her sons, with whom she finally agreed to live. Grishin cunningly structured her share of Arumov's fund to reward her for living with family.

He could not, he told her with a satanic sparkle in his eyes, justify giving her a large stipend whilst she enjoyed established circumstances in Moscow, but living with five grandchildren would involve many more expenses, which he was honour-bound to meet.

Mironov was most impressed with this Machiavellian acrobatic, especially after Natalya Fedorovna sadly nodded in consent, absorbing this performance with knowing acquiescence. It was not the money but the strength of the man's conviction – anyone who knew Grishin respected and trusted his judgement absolutely.

The other operatives returned to their homes all over Russia to catch up on the season's drinking. The idea was that the money would not begin to flow for a few years, save in emergencies. If the authorities stated their desire not to seek, it would be unwise to work at being found.

All former *spetznaz* servicemen remain in the army reserve – even in middle age their experience makes them invaluable as instructors. It was relatively easy for a simple breach of security to return a list of men who served with Mironov, all of them now targets for any future reprisal.

Alas, their records met with something of an accident.

They were weeded to remove the files of men killed in action or deceased since leaving active service. But a careless error resulted in the files of those still living being moved to another storage facility, leaving the deceased files instead. Anyone specifically seeking former members of Mironov's team would find the conversation very one-sided.

For reasons that would never be fully elucidated, the records of living men were filed amongst those of a reserve artillery company, and the computer classification of each file was changed accordingly. Still eligible for pensions and reserve call-up, they would be absolutely impossible to associate with Berezov's demise.

Mironov was reasonably sure that he left no loose ends apart from himself.

It was well past midnight when they found themselves outside Nina's apartment block, numb with cold and gratefully tired.

Nina slowly inserted the key, wiggled it until the imprecise copy found the pins and leaned into the steel door with her shoulder. Mironov added the force of his arm, and the armoured contraption swung on its crude hinges.

They walked into the sour warmth of the vestibule and summoned the lift. By then Nina was swaying on her feet, and Mironov caught her shoulders and pressed her to his chest. She rested her head on his shoulder until the lift arrived, and they boarded it without parting.

That was how they rode towards the top of the building, emerging from the lift and slowly walking to the door, still taking care not to break contact between their bodies.

Nina opened her front door and looked at

Mironov. He nodded with reassurance, and they entered the apartment with resolve. He shut the door with a backward slide of his elbow.

Nina's strength ebbed once they were inside. She slid down to kneel on the floor and covered her face with both hands. Mironov picked her up and carried her to the bed.

The bedroom was just as she left it after fleeing from Berezov's thugs. Some clothes were strewn over the floor, and the window was opened slightly, filling the bedroom with pure cold air.

He laid Nina on the bed and took off her boots. She instantly fell asleep, and he covered her with a woollen plaid from one of the closets. Mironov watched over her for a while and, satisfied that she didn't stir, left to have a shower.

In the bathroom he tore off the uniform, suddenly aware of its coarseness and weight. He left it in a crumpled heap on the floor and climbed into the shower.

He stood under hot water and cleansed himself of his last mission. It was possible, he thought, that time might allow the rest of his memories to be cleansed as well.

A new man emerged from the shower in a muscled body of a former assassin.

Viktor rubbed himself dry with a towel that faintly smelled of Nina's perfume and padded back to the bedroom. She was deeply asleep, a woman released from her torment and left utterly spent.

He climbed under the prickly blanket and embraced her warmth, feeling her shift to press against him. Her cold hand retracted under the blanket and tenderly took hold of his wrist. His thoughts dissolved in the swirl of fatigue, acceptance and release.

Then Viktor awoke in the uncertain light of a February morning. He remained in Nina's tight embrace, right arm resting on her shoulders.

He lay still for a long time, staring into her forehead, smelling her hair and feeling her move as she breathed softly in her sleep.

Then came that magic moment when she shuddered slightly, took in a deep breath and came awake. He felt her tense as she remembered where she was, then her soft hand caressed his forearm.

For a while they savoured their embrace. Then came the morning sun, its furtive rays piercing the morning and firing the bedroom with a soft golden glow.

Nina rose on her elbow and stared at him, her gaze now steady and profound. She was the most beautiful sight of his miserable life, Viktor realized with elation. Even the tears that welled in her eyes had tiny reflections of the morning sun. Small bequests from that which gives life, they were military decorations of a woman whose courage defied Viktor's imagination.

They joined in a kiss that lasted forever, and the salt of her tears displaced the stale flavours of dust, cordite and blood that once comprised his existence.

She ran her hand down the back of his neck and pressed him closer. Viktor felt her heat as her leg slid over his hips, and she was suddenly on top, her mouth still pressed to his. He completed the movement, rolling over onto his back.

Nina caressed his heavy shoulders and rested her head on his chest, staying still for a while.

At length she tore away, wiping her eyes with the back of her hand, and Viktor felt the rising rhythm of her body. He responded, a timeless repetition of life's eternal rite enveloping their senses.

Afterwards they were complete, their still repose a celebration of everything that draws living beings back from the void.

IBE
2002-2006

A BOOK BY THE SAME AUTHOR:

TRAIL OF AN INCUBUS
EnglinSolutions Ltd NZ ® 2005
Distributed in association with www.amazon.com

Written in 2000, this book is set in contemporary Australia – a mature society with a defined cultural identity but not without rough edges, which make lives unnecessarily hard and complicated.

Into this landscape drifts a demonic figure who calls himself Darius, who first appears in a short prologue, set in Southern Germany in the closing days of World War II.

It turns out that alongside humans there exists another race, outwardly human but with far greater longevity and physical strength. Their intelligence is about the same or greater than human, albeit it with certain blind spots. They hate humanity for displacing them from the top of the food chain, and their character traits give rise to traditional demonic myths - an enemy moving amongst us, intelligent, resourceful and hostile – and in constant search for human virgins.

But Darius does not merely wish to reproduce – he hopes that humanity is now such a self-evident failure, that it is possible to find women who will be willing accomplices in rebuilding his race and overthrow humans as the dominant species. He ruthlessly pursues this goal with all means at his disposal. Darius behaves as a magnet - all who meet him instinctively line up to serve him or to oppose him. But time is on his side.